Marianne Bailey - Wickham
April 2014

SEARCHING *for* ANGELS

The story of a young girl brought up in foster care

MARIANNE BAILEY-WICKHAM

authorHOUSE®

AuthorHouse™ UK Ltd.
1663 Liberty Drive
Bloomington, IN 47403 USA
www.authorhouse.co.uk
Phone: 0800.197.4150

Published by AuthorHouse   03/11/2014

ISBN: 978-1-4918-9873-4 (sc)
ISBN: 978-1-4918-9885-7 (e)

Dedication

To my four beautiful children
A, V, N and D
Thank you for just being you!

OVERTURE

I am Laura-Louise and this is my story. I write it now because there is so much that I might forget and so much more that I would ***rather*** forget.

This is my attempt to make sense of the chaos:

My search for angels.

CHAPTER 1

We wept buckets when Grandma told us the news. We snuggled up, one on either side of her in the big bed with the brown, flowery duvet. We wiped our tears and threw our soggy tissues into the chamber pot.

I knew that life would never be the same again but I had no idea how dramatically everything would change. I really thought that Andrew, my big brother and I would have continued living in the same house, perhaps with Grandma too. We'd have managed. I knew we would. I was six and he was seven. But Grandma said that we had to move.

"So can we come and live with you then?" I asked. She was silent for a moment. I didn't understand the problem. We had all stayed with her lots of times. Happy holidays. She had a big house at the seaside. "There's plenty of room." I urged. She remained silent and thoughtful. "And we'd be good."

"I couldn't." she sighed. I love you both lots and lots but I couldn't . . . . I *couldn't* have you come and live with me. I'm too old. I'm over sixty now. When you are both teenagers I shall be in my seventies. I'm much too old. You wouldn't be happy. I couldn't cope."

I didn't understand. Sixty, seventy . . . . what did that have to do with it?

Perhaps, I thought we could go and live with our father.

We didn't know him very well but Mother wouldn't have liked it. Later that day an old Aunt that I had never met before came to see us. She gave me a big hug and a slobbery kiss. She scared me and I cried again. Andrew hid in the garden. She gave us huge chocolate Easter eggs, some yellow flowers and some paper money in a purse. I think it was a lot of money. Grandma said that she would look after it.

I knew what it meant to die. Our kitten had died. I never saw him again. Now I would never see Mother again. Never. Thirty years on I still weep when I remember that moment. I remember my father but we hardly ever saw him. He made Mother unhappy. She was glad when he went.

The day that we moved out of our home was horrible. Andrew hugged the cushions and kissed the walls. Grandma packed our clothes into suitcases. She didn't know what things fitted. There was my blue knitted dress. I used to love it but now I hated it as I watched it packed into the case. I didn't know where we were going. Andrew didn't say much. He didn't even cry now. He hit me when I tried to speak to him about Mother. Grandma packed some old photographs for us. She kept talking, just talking without really saying anything or maybe I was just not listening.

We were going to stay at my friend's house. It was my friend Katy from school, her brother David and their Mum and Dad. We'd stayed there once before when Mother was in hospital. They only lived around the corner. Some strange grown-ups came and talked to us. A lady said that she was a Social Worker. We could live with a foster family. She said that she had seen our Dad. He wanted to see us sometimes and buy us presents but he had another family now. He had his own life. He didn't have room in his life for us. And so we moved to stay with the foster family, the Taylors. It all happened so quickly. I pushed my dolls' pram. Andrew drove his go-kart. Grandma walked behind with the suitcases.

"Mind the road Andrew! Keep hold of that pram Laura-Louise! Be careful! Wait for me!" It was April and I carried our silver Christmas tree balanced across the dolls' pram. Mrs. Taylor was at the door to greet us. She was smiling

"What shall we call our new parents?" I asked Grandma but foster Mum replied.

"You can call me Mary . . . or Mum, if you like."

I desperately wanted to feel part of the family. I called them Mum and Dad from the second I walked in the door. Andrew called her Mary. He never did call her Mum. I carried the huge suitcase up the stairs on my own while the others were talking. Grandma hugged us again. She smelled of cigarettes and fennel tea. She got out her camera and took a photograph of us with our new family. She gave us our purses with some money, then she said 'Goodbye' and left. We were alone yet not alone.

The first day with our foster family was strange. Suddenly my whole world had collapsed. Now I had a new Mum and Dad, a sister called Katy and a little brother called David. I liked having a little brother. I'd always been the youngest at home. I tried to pick him up but he kicked me. There was a swing in the garden. I pushed David on the swing. I made him go really high. He liked it but his Mum didn't. Then Andrew pushed him on the swing. He made the swing go round and round. The rope went round

David's neck. Andrew laughed. David coughed. The rope went tighter and tighter. Suddenly New Mum screamed and shouted at Andrew. He cried. She un-spun the rope and picked up David. He had big, red rope burns on his neck. New Mum was cross. I was cross. Andrew didn't know what he'd done wrong. He was only playing and he hadn't pushed the swing up high. He sat on the swing rocking gently and talking, mumbling to himself.

"I'm praying." he explained.

"That's good." said New Mum. "It will help."

"I'm praying to my Mum."

"You can pray to God." said Mum. We didn't understand.

"She's still here," he whispered secretly to me later. "They don't know it but she's still here . . . with me." He touched his chest near where his heart might be. "I talk to her. She never said 'Goodbye' . . . so she's still here." And then he sobbed. "I saw her," he said through the tears. "I saw her in the garden at home before we left. Just a little ball of light hovering by the bush, then she flew away. I saw her. It *was* her. It was her way of saying 'goodbye'. He sobbed again. I should have hugged him but I didn't.

It was the sort of day when no-one seemed to know what to do so we all went shopping. I took my purse with all the money and I held New Mum's hand. Andrew was very quiet. We looked at the beds in a big furniture shop.

"Can I spend my money in here?" I asked.

"No Dear. Not in here."

The man in the furniture shop came up to serve us. Andrew stared at him and said,

"Guess what happened on Saturday." The man smiled.

"Mmm . . . . I don't know. What happened on Saturday?" He clearly expected an answer like 'It was my birthday!' or 'We went to the zoo!'

"My Mum died." said Andrew matter-of-factly. It sounded as though it was the most natural thing in the world for a seven-year old to say to a shop keeper. New Mum tried to explain that that was why we needed to buy new beds but the man had gone. He had a white handkerchief in his hand.

Next we went to Woolworth's. I looked at the toys.

"Can I spend my money in here? I could buy that big, fluffy rabbit."

"No Dear. Not in here."

We went to the newsagents.

"Can I spend my money in here? I could buy that big book **and** that box of chocolates."

"No Dear. You must save your money. Don't waste it on silly things."

"We went in the gardening shop."

"Can I spend my money in here? I could buy some seeds."

"Yes!" exclaimed Mum unexpectedly, in a moment's inspiration. "Why Yes! What a good idea Laura-Louise! You could buy some seeds." We all spent ages choosing but it proved to be a brilliant idea. I chose lettuce seeds, Andrew got some Spring onions, Katy got some beetroot and David bought radishes. It was a strange choice. Back in our new garden we were each given a plot to plant our seeds. It gave me a stake in the land that was especially mine. It gave me something to look forward to as I watered and tended my own patch.

In the afternoon we all went with New Mum to her 'Women's Meeting' at the church. There were some other children there. The ladies were very old and wrinkly but they were kind to us.

"Guess what happened on Saturday?" Andrew asked again.

"Tell me." said the kind, grey-haired lady.

"My Mum died." She hugged him first then she hugged me second.

That evening New Dad came home from work. He kissed Mum. Andrew sniggered. We weren't used to seeing grown ups kiss except on television. Then Dad kissed each of us in turn. We had tea and watched a funny cartoon programme. It was like being a normal family. I sat on Mum's lap and she sang a silly song about 'Row your boat.' It made me laugh. Bedtime could have been difficult but I was going to share a room with Katy so I was quite looking forward to having someone to talk to in the night. I knew her quite well. She was in my class at school. She used to be my friend. Now, I supposed, she was my sister. As I lay in bed listening to her rhythmic breathing I could hear the grownups talking downstairs. I couldn't hear what they were saying but I guessed they were talking about me. I tried to listen. Under the covers I clutched my favourite doll to my chest. My Real Dad had bought it for me. It was very beautiful and had cost a lot of money he'd said. Over the next few weeks we waited for our seeds to grow and there I developed a fascination for growing things . . . and I still love salad! The seeds were a stroke of genius and it had all been ***my*** idea in the first place.

And so the days passed as we settled into the 'honeymoon period' with our new family. I often dreamed about Mother and I sometimes thought that one day, when all this is over, we will get back to normal. But then I knew, I knew deep down that it would never be.

Dads leave. Mums die. Life goes on.

NOCTURNE

"Laura-Louise! Laura-Louise!" I sit lazily relaxed in an old, overgrown garden, amidst tall, waving grasses. Rays of sunlight filter through the trees creating mysterious shadows moving in silent accompaniment to my dreams. I watch the ants busy in the warmth of Summer. Ants have a purpose in life. They know where they are going. I gaze upwards to clear, blue skies. Bubbles of gold float by filling the emptiness.

"Laura-Louise! Laura-Louise! Come in now! Tea's ready!" I rise from my thoughts and follow the golden bubbles drifting through the open back door towards my mother's voice. She sounds young, yet frail and far away. The tea table is laid with embroidered tablecloth and laden with tossed green salad in a green, lettuce-leaf bowl. There are carved wooden salad-servers, salt, vinegar and salad cream. There is home-made cake and cream cakes. Best china plates and cups and saucers are placed neatly in settings.

"Have we got visitors? Have we got visitors?"

"Laura-Louise! Laura-L . . . ." My mother's voice is fading. Golden bubbles float over the tea table. I stretch out my hand to take a cake. Black ants run over my fingers and palm. They crawl diligently over the tablecloth between the plates of food. Hundreds, now thousands of them until the whole table is a seething, black mass.

"Laura-Louise!" Her voice trails into silence.

"Mummy!" I scream. "Don't go away!"

Then the golden bubbles burst.

CHAPTER 2

The Easter holidays ended and we went back to school. New Mum wrote letters to our teachers to explain that our mother had died during the holidays. The message soon went round the school amongst friends and staff. In class I had to write about 'What I did in the holidays.' (Where do teachers get all these original ideas?!) I wrote in my book:

'I had a lovely holiday.'

At playtime I held the teacher's hand. At dinner time I held the dinner-lady's hand. She was nice to me. She gave me sweets and didn't tell me off when I couldn't eat my dinner. My friends wanted to know what had happened to my Mum. They began to ask questions. They wanted details. 'How did she die? Did you go to her funeral? What happens when you die? What's it like to see a dead person? Is it a skeleton?' I didn't know what to say. I couldn't answer their questions and until then I hadn't even thought about her funeral. I know now that Grandma wouldn't let us go. She wanted us to remember Mother as she was . . . pretty, blond, vivacious and loving. Now, with the wisdom that comes with retrospect and adulthood, I think we would have benefited from a formal 'Farewell.' I never had the chance to say 'Goodbye and Thanks Mum.' I regret that.

Andrew and I settled surprisingly well into our new family. Katy and I played endless games with our dolls. It was good having a sister, well, most of the time anyway. We went to ballet classes and Brownies together and we all had music lessons. I was learning to play the piano. Andrew and David went to a Boys' Club but they didn't play together much. I began to feel happy. It was all too good . . . ***too*** happy. I shouldn't be happy. I waited for the bubble to burst.

One evening Grandma came to see us. She had something to tell us, just Andrew and me. She sounded serious. We sat down facing her. Andrew picked up a cushion and wrapped his arms comfortingly round it. I looked for some diversion so bent down to stroke the old, white cat as she wandered past. Grandma held a mug of strong, black coffee in both hands.

"I've got a surprise for you." she began. "I don't know whether you will think it a nice surprise or not." We didn't speak. I stroked the cat again and prepared myself for more bad news. Whatever could have happened now? She continued.

"Did you know that your mother had been married before? Before she met your father?" Andrew nodded but I didn't remember ever hearing anything about it.

"She was married to a man called Robert and she had two children before she had you."

I sat up straight and looked at her. Was she joking? It was not the sort of thing that she joked about.

"You have another brother and sister. Well, ***half*** brother and sister. They are teenagers now and they know about you. They'd like to meet you. What do you think Dears?"

I came to me as a huge shock. I had thought that we were special to Mother,—just Andrew and me. If she had had other children before us it seemed as though we were being pushed further out of the family, demoted and de-based. I felt humiliated. How had she lied to us all those years?

Andrew spoke up.

"Have I got a teenage brother then?"

"Yes Love."

"Does he play football?"

"I expect so." Grandma smiled.

"What's his name?"

"His name is Robbie and he is sixteen. He'd love to meet you Andrew. He lives a long way away."

"Does he live in Australia? . . . . Or Penzance? That's a long way."

"No Darling. He only lives in London. Would you like to meet them?"

Grandma sounded calm and just a little sad. She waited for my reaction. Andrew seemed excited but I wasn't so sure. I smiled and nodded anyway.

"I'm so pleased." She sighed. "I wasn't sure how you'd take the news."

This news apparently prompted a letter from our Real Dad. He wanted to see us too. He said that he had borrowed some money and was moving to a bigger house. Maybe he had room in his life for us to live with him. He said there was going to be a court case to decide where we were going to live. No-one asked me what I thought.

We went to meet Mother's first husband. He was nice. He made jokes and made me laugh. Our newly discovered half-brother and sister were lovely. I was surprised that I liked them. Everyone said that I looked just like Jenny.

Andrew and Robbie were great friends from the second they met. They played football and had fun-fights romping round the garden. Andrew idolised Robbie. He loved having a big brother hero. One of their play fights resulted in a suspected broken arm and Andrew being rushed to hospital in a panic. X-rays proved that all was well. Robbie was reprimanded and told that he didn't know his own strength. Jenny was fun and confident at fourteen years. She reminded me of Mother. I held her hand. She seemed so grown up.

"Can we come and live with you?" I whispered to her. I'd like to live here with you." She was quiet.

"Er . . . I don't know. I'd have to ask." She let go of my hand.

"Then let's ask. Now."

"Can we come and live here with you?" I asked optimistically.

But it couldn't be. They tried to explain that they were a family now with *their* new Mum and two more children. They told us that we *had* a family, a foster family and our place was there with them. That was where we belonged at least until the court case. But they did have something very special to give us. Andrew and I were each handed an envelope. Inside was a letter written by our mother just before she died. I recognised her writing.

> To all my dear children, Robbie, Jenny, Andrew and
> Laura—Louise.
> You have given me more love and more happiness
> than anyone else in my life.
> I don't want to leave you, not for the world, but I
> know I will soon be gone.

Work hard. Always be kind and polite and look after each other.
Always remember that I love you very, very much.
God bless you,
Mum xxxx

Robbie, as the eldest had the original and the rest of us were given photo-copies. I still carry that letter close to me. It has become very tattered but remains very precious. Sometimes I get it out and tearfully read it, especially when things get hard. I read it and remember my beautiful Mother who loved me so much. I still miss her and I think how different my life would have been if there had been a cure for cancer.

It seemed that our short visit to Robbie and Jenny stirred up bad feelings amongst the rest of the family. The pending court case put us all on edge. Our foster family was feeling the strain.

One day I borrowed Katy's 'Peter Rabbit' book. I didn't ask her. She had a whole shelf full of them. I love rabbits. Still do. It was a beautiful book with lovely pictures. I knew it was special. Katy had had it since she was a baby. I think an old Aunt had bought them for her. I sat on the floor in our bedroom on my own flicking over the pages, looking at the pictures. Then Katy came in and saw me. Well, I didn't think she'd mind. She didn't speak, just gave a haughty sniff, snatched the book which ripped apart and then went to tell Mum. Katy was angry. So was I. So was Mum. The book had split into two completely separate parts. It broke at page fourteen and my favourite picture of Mrs. Rabbit with her shopping basket and umbrella. Mum was so cross with me.

"It was a special book." she snapped. "Katy has looked

after it all these years and YOU have torn it. Look at it! Look at it! It is completely ruined!" She shouted and pushed the book towards me. A corner of the page went in my eye. I didn't know what to do. People had been so kind to me until that moment. Why couldn't we be a family again? Mum went on and on about the book.

"You have absolutely ruined a very precious book. The whole collection is ruined. You cannot be trusted. Didn't your mother ever teach you how to look after things?"

That was it. The mention of my mother was too much. I stormed out of the room, slammed the door and determined to get my revenge on Katy. Sibling rivalry was nothing compared to my feelings at that moment.

The honeymoon period was over.

CHAPTER 3

Our Real Dad heard the news that we had visited Big Robbie and Jenny, our half siblings. He was not happy. He was coming to see us. I longed to see him with such a passion that I ached inside. It was all arranged. He would pick us up on Saturday at nine o'clock in the morning.

We were excited. Mum washed us, brushed us and dressed us in best clothes. I was outside the house waiting at ten to nine. I watched every car as it came round the bend. I wondered what he would look like now. Nine o'clock came.

. . . . And went . . . . then quarter past nine.

"I expect he's stuck in traffic." I said.

By half past nine Mum was worried about us.

"Come inside and wait." she said. "You can watch out of the window."

I didn't want to go in but Andrew did. He was never any good at waiting. I stayed outside watching every car.

"Maybe he has broken down," I muttered, "Or lost his watch. He did that once before. I remember. He couldn't find his watch and I found it in the bathroom."

I could have gone on making excuses for him.

He arrived at eleven o'clock. He was sorry he was late. We climbed into the back of the car.

"It's a lovely big car." I exclaimed. "It smells nice."

"It's new." explained our father. "It smells of leather. Cost me a pretty penny I can tell you."

"Where are we going?" I asked. "Can we go to your house?"

"I can't stay for long." He avoided my questions.

"But where *are* we going? I'd love to go to your house."

"We're going into town."

He took us to the hairdresser's. He said that my hair was a mess. It was too long and he asked the hairdresser to cut it.

"Not too short please . . . ." I objected quietly.

Andrew had his hair cut too. We got back in the car.

"Where are we going now?"

Dad was silent. I sat in the back seat looking at him as he drove. He was wearing an orange sleeveless T shirt that showed off his suntan. I noticed his muscles. I remembered the time when we all lived together as an ordinary family. He flexed his muscles. I'd seen him do that before.

"Dad," I said.

"Mmm."

"Dad, could we come and live with you?"

"Is that what you'd like?"

"Yes, please."

"What about you Andrew? You are very quiet."

"Don't know." he shrugged.

"Well you better get thinking about it and don't shrug like that. You are picking up bad habits. Listen kids. There is going to be a court case and I think that your place is with me, but not just yet. I haven't got room for you just now. Your mother shouldn't have died when she did."

"She couldn't help it Dad. She didn't want to die. She said so in her letter."

16

"What letter?" he snapped. He sounded angry. I could never understand grown ups.

"But *could* we come and live with you?"

"Listen, I'm trying to get some more money so that I can get a bigger house then you *will* both come and live with me and Kirsten and our children. But don't tell anyone. Not yet. It's our secret remember. You are good at keeping secrets aren't you Sweetheart.

Do you remember our little secret?"

I remembered. It was painful. "I won't tell anyone." I began to sob.

"Promise?"

I promised.

"Promise on your Mother's grave?"

He drove us home. Yes, *home* . . . . to our foster family. Andrew just jumped out of the car and ran indoors. I stayed behind in the car and wiped my tears on my sleeve. Dad put his arm round me and kissed me. I could smell the warmth of his body touching me.

"Remember our secrets. Never, ever tell."

"No Dad. Will you come again?"

"I'll come if they let me."

"Bye Dad!"

"Bye bye, Sweetheart."

I waved as I watched him drive away and wiped away another tear. I looked at the house. So this was *home* now was it? Andrew had already helped himself to a drink and a biscuit. He had made himself at home. Mum passed a drink to me and offered me the biscuit tin.

"Your hair looks nice." She said politely. "Where did you go?"

"To the hairdresser's." I replied unnecessarily. "The expensive one in the shopping centre. My father says that he'll take us there again in six weeks. He's going to write you a letter about it."

"Oh," replied Mum. "Did you have a good time?"

Andrew sipped his drink and began to speak.

"My Dad's very strong. He's in the Army. He's got a gun. He's going to show it to me one day. It's one of the biggest guns in the whole army."

"Really?" said Mum but I knew she was only pretending to sound interested. "Uncle Len used to be in the Army too but a long time ago."

"Cor! Was he?" Andrew sat up. "Did he ever get killed or anything?" Mum laughed. We all laughed but I wasn't sure why.

"He'll tell you all about it when he gets home." she said.

I went upstairs to find Katy. She was surprised to see me back so soon.

"I thought you were staying out all day with your real Dad. Mum was going to take us two out somewhere special. Just us. I s'pose we can't go now *you're* back." We played a game with our dolls.

The broken 'Peter Rabbit' book was still there. I tried not to look at it but somehow my eyes were constantly drawn towards the glaring, ripped pages. I didn't say anything and I really think that Katy had forgotten all about it.

My own birthday was coming soon. I would be seven. I wondered what this new family did about birthdays. My mother had been too ill last year to have parties. I'd love a party. I could invite lots of people from school, perhaps the whole class, everyone! Then I'd have lots of friends. I looked at Katy and her prettiness. She was tall and thin with long fair, fly-away hair. My hair is thick and dark and shiny. I am short and still have a weight problem even now. Grandma used to tell me that I have the 'family bum.' It sounded funny but I was never satisfied with my size and shape. I thought that eating salads would make me slim and pretty.

I asked Mum about my seventh birthday.

"Can I invite some friends round please?"

"Would you like a party?"

"O yes please! With cake and games and lots of friends?"

And so the party was arranged. I wasn't allowed to invite the whole class, just ten of them. The children from next door came too and two of Katy's friends that I didn't know. I soon got to know them and then they played with me more than Katy. It was early May and the cake looked like a maypole with jelly babies dancing round holding the ribbons. My Real Dad sent me a huge card. It said:

'To My Dearest Daughter.'

There was a brown paper parcel with it and inside was the most gorgeous dress in creamy Victorian lace and cotton with frills and flowers and puffy sleeves. Katy just looked at it. I could tell that she had never, ever had a dress so beautiful. I wore it at my party and all my friends admired it and asked where I got it. I was proud to say that my Real Dad bought it for me. I had just loads and loads of presents, some from Aunts that had known my mother but I had never heard of them They sent me money too. I had lots of money.

It was a good party. We played funny games and Dad told jokes and made us all laugh. I was sorry when it was all over. I wanted it to go on for ever but I had to wave goodbye to everyone and we went inside. There was such a muddle.

"Thank you for my party Mum." I said politely.

"What a good girl you are! But look at all this mess."

"I'll do all the clearing up." I promised optimistically.

"We'll do it together." Mum said.

Even Andrew picked up a tea towel to help.

"When it's my b . . . b . . . birthday," he stuttered. "Can I have a p . . . party too?"

"Of course you can!" promised Mum.

"But I don't want a cake like a m . . . m . . . maypole."

"What would you like?"

"Could I have Superman . . . or a television?"

"O dear! I'll try!"

Andrew was usually quiet but he had become more and more withdrawn since we had lived with the foster family. He didn't speak much and when he did I noticed that he sometimes stammered and the words he wanted to say wouldn't come out straight.

I tried to talk to him about our mother but he didn't have much to say. I think he felt guilty as though we shouldn't speak about her now so I stopped trying and made up my mind to become a part of this new family. I wanted them to accept me and love me as much as they loved Katy and little David.

Mum was worried about Andrew too. One day I told

20

her that he used to have to go to the hospital to have his ears tested. She seemed surprised. She didn't know and said that she would find out about it. In time, an appointment was made for him to have a hearing test. We were all shocked to find out that he had less than seventy per cent hearing in both ears. He would need an operation to fit grommets in his ears. It sounded scary and I could tell that Andrew was worried. He didn't like hospitals. Our mother had gone into hospital and she never came out.

CHAPTER 4

Andrew's birthday came next. He was eight and we had another party. He invited two friends from school. I invited my friends too but Mum said that it was Andrew's party so his friends came first. He had a cake with a Superman picture on the top and we watched a cartoon on television. He had lots of presents from old Aunts.

The day after the party a brown envelope arrived with a letter from the hospital. There was a date for Andrew's ear operation and two days after that a package arrived for him from our Real Dad. There was a huge card and a big, red, radio-controlled model car. We all followed as he drove it around the dining room and into the kitchen and through the lounge. I could see that David wanted a go, actually we all did. Dad had a go then Andrew packed it away in its box. He read the letter from the hospital again.

School was going well. I had lots of friends. I wanted to do well so I worked hard and the teacher was pleased with me. I got good reports. I wanted lots of friends but I liked to stay close to the grown-ups. I desperately wanted to feel that I *belonged.* We all need to be loved but for me it became a mission that engulfed every thought, every relationship, every moment of every day. It was the be all and end all of Life.

Our foster family was always busy. Dad went out to work early every morning before we were awake. Mum saw us off to school after a hurried breakfast. She always fussed over David because he was the youngest and still in the Infants Classes. She did his shoes up for him and tucked in his shirt and walked him to school. I quickly learned to get myself ready. I sorted my own school clothes and brushed my thick, dark hair. In fact I didn't want Mum to touch my hair and I resented her washing and ironing my clothes especially the ones that my Real Mum had bought me. I became fearfully independent. I could manage. I *would* manage.

Mum went to work part-time too. She was a teacher in a primary school but she was always there to meet us when we came home from school. Evenings were often busy with Brownies, ballet, the children's club at the church and visiting friends. And so the days rolled on.

When Andrew went into hospital I was worried about him. There was a young man at the church who worked at the hospital. He was nice. He changed his hours especially so that he could be on duty in the theatre while Andrew had his operation. I had to go to school. I had a spelling test but my thoughts were with my brother. He was the one person in my life who had always been there and I didn't want to lose him. We all went to visit him in the evening. He was sitting up in bed and smiling. He told us that our Real Dad had been to see him and given him a little battery-operated game. I was surprised and I could see that Mum and Dad were shocked too.

"We had to tell him that you were in hospital." Mum explained. "He needed to know."

Andrew seemed happy and quite well. I just wished that I had seen my Real Dad too. It wasn't fair. I wondered if I were ill, would he come to visit me?

Andrew made a good recovery and was soon home again. I prayed to God that he would get better but then I had prayed to God that my Mum would get better. I prayed so earnestly. So why had she died when I needed her? I must have been very bad. Now I was trying hard to be good.

"Does God answer our prayers?" I asked Mum one day.

"God always answers our prayers." she replied.

"So why did my Mum die?"

"We don't always understand why God does things the way he does. We just have to trust him that he knows best. He always answers our prayers. It's just that sometimes the answer is 'No'."

I didn't understand. Maybe God was the answer to all my problems. Andrew had got better and come home. I decided to pray more often. Somehow I felt closer to my Real Mum when I prayed. I wondered if I could tell God the special secret but I had promised Real Dad that I would never, ever tell anyone. I kept it to myself.

Andrew's hearing had suddenly improved.

"What's that bubbly sound?" he asked one afternoon. We didn't know. Perhaps something had gone wrong with his ears again.

"What *is* that bubbly sound? I can hear it. It's coming from . . . . over there!"

He pointed to the fish tank. Then I realised what it was.

"It's the bubbles in the fish tank!" I exclaimed. "It's just that you've never been able to hear them before." We were all so used to the sound that we never really noticed it. We all laughed. Andrew's operation was a milestone and with his improved hearing came his greater self-confidence. As he began to blossom, so I withdrew. I needed to find a reason for being alive. My mother had died but I was still alive and I wanted to know why.

The next milestone was the court case. The best part of that was the arrival of Grandma. I was so pleased to see her again. She stayed with some Aunts but came to see us every day. She talked to us. Really **talked.** Grandma was good at talking and she said important things. She talked to us about our mother and I suddenly realised that she missed her too. We had lost a mother but somehow I had almost forgotten that she had lost her only daughter. Her only child.

"You don't expect to bury your children." she said one day. She was still grieving but at least she could talk about it. I couldn't.

Grandma was lovely, wrinkled, kind and full of wisdom. She took us shopping. Just Andrew and me. It was almost like being a family again. I felt special. She bought us new shoes and Andrew needed new school shirts. I needed a pink cardigan for ballet class and Grandma said that she would knit one for me. Katy already had one. She took us to a coffee shop and we all sat at a big, round table sipping our hot drinks and munching chocolate cake.

Andrew asked her about the court case. I wanted to know too but didn't like to ask. He was getting braver than me. She explained it all so clearly.

"Your father, that's your Real Dad, says he wants you to go and live with him. He has written lots of letters, but I promised your Mother on her death bed that I would be your legal guardian until you . . . ."

"What's a Leak-o-Guardian?" interrupted Andrew. "Is it a sort of Guardian Angel?"

"No!" smiled Grandma. "I am your **Legal** Guardian. It just means that I am responsible for you. I have to see that you are well looked after and happy that's why I think it is best for you to stay where you are with the same foster family. They have been very good to you."

"Yes," said Andrew. "So you are **like** a Guardian Angel! I want us to stay where we are now. I don't want to move again." He was doing most of the talking and I stayed quiet.

"What about you, Laura-Louise? What do you think?" She looked closely at me. I dropped my eyes and fiddled with my coffee spoon. I looked at my reflection. I turned the spoon over and my reflection turned upside down. Everything was upside-down but I didn't have an answer to her question.

"Tell me what you think." she urged. "I need to know what you think." Grandma leaned forward and spoke quietly, seriously. "You see," she went on, "Your father has said that you **asked** if you could live with him. He thinks you are unhappy. Are you unhappy? Did you ask to go and live with him?"

I looked at the upside down world.

Grandma spoke again even more seriously. "That is why we have a court case. We are going to decide where you will live."

I started to cry. So this big 'court-case' thing was all my fault. I didn't know what I wanted. I didn't even know if I was happy or sad. Grandma fumbled in her bag for a tissue. She handed it to me.

"Wipe your eyes Darling. Please tell me what you think. That big hole in your face is called a mouth. It is there to let out all the things that are going on in your head." I started to laugh through my tears. "Don't keep it all to yourself. Try to let people know what you think."

"Can't we come and live with you?" I sniffed.

"I'm sorry." she replied. "I've tried to explain before. I know that it is hard for you to understand. I'm too old. I couldn't cope. If you did come to live with me you would have to change schools and you'd have no friends there."

I wanted friends.

"If we stay where we are will you still come to visit?"

"Of course I will! And you can come and stay with me in the holidays and I will telephone you every Friday and I will send you postcards and letters every week. I love you lots and lots and I want what is the very, very best for you."

"And will our Real Dad be allowed to come and see us too?" I asked the question cautiously as I was afraid of the answer.

"Yes! I'm sure he will want that and I will never stop him from seeing you. So my Dear, tell me honestly, what do you really want?"

"I want to stay where I am with Mary and Len and Katy and David. Oh . . . and Andrew of course. Especially Andrew I've got to be where he is. And anyway, my lettuce seeds are growing well and we're going to have salad for tea."

"O.K." said Grandma. "Come on, let's go ***home!***"

CHAPTER 5

*"C**hildren in private Foster Care are not protected.***" the lady had said.

It was the day of the Court Case and I didn't know what to expect. Mum and Dad were tense, talking to each other over breakfast but not to me. I felt it. Grandma arrived, wearing a very smart green suit with a neat black and white scarf. Her spectacles hung on a cord around her neck. She joined us at the table and helped herself to toast and marmalade. I watched the crumbs land in her glasses like a baby's crumb-catcher. I didn't know what to do. I was surprised when I was told to go upstairs and put on my school uniform. I was silent. Andrew looked puzzled.

"But I thought we were going to the Case-court!" he shouted angrily.

*"**Court** Case."* corrected Mum. "It's a *Court* Case and yes we are going. *We* are going but *you* are all going to school. *You* don't need to be there. So hurry up and get ready or you'll make us all late."

"Bum!" screamed Andrew. "Bum, bum, bum, bum, bum . . . ." I think it was the rudest word he could think of at the time. He knew it would make Mum cross. He banged his breakfast plate down on the table and then he thought of an even ruder word. He shouted. The plate smashed. I laughed at his words. It made me want to giggle. Katy and little David laughed too as Andrew stormed out of the room and slammed the door.

"I ain't gonna go to boring old school!" he shouted from the stairs.

I looked at Mum and Grandma. They were all there. Even Dad was there this morning. He hadn't gone to work. I tried to smile.

"I'll get ready for school." I said meekly.

I kissed Mum and Dad and Grandma and left the room. I walked slowly up the stairs past Andrew who was still sitting on the bottom step. I looked at him surreptitiously to see if he was crying. He wasn't, but his face was so red I couldn't see his freckles. He pulled his jumper up over his head and grunted as I passed. I went on up the stairs and started to get ready for school. I thought they'd all be pleased with me. I did everything I could to try to please them. While I dressed I could hear Grandma talking to Andrew on the stairs. She was sitting beside him. I couldn't hear all they were saying but eventually Andrew came calmly up to his room. In silence he got ready for school. I wrote a little note. It said: 'I love you Grandma' and I drew a picture of a smiling rabbit and a heart. I pushed it into her hand as we said Goodbye and went out the door. We all left as though it was a perfectly normal day. The sun was shining and I could smell Summer. I met some friends from class and we stood watching the noisy tractor-mower cutting the grass on the school field.

The slow, familiar routine of the school timetable was comforting. I saw Andrew at dinner time. He was playing football on the field. He had green skid marks on his new white shirt. He was laughing as though he had forgotten all about the court case. I tried to forget it too but the more I tried the bigger it became in my head. I was just a young girl stuck in life; a life I did not choose. Money buys freedom,—the freedom to choose. I know that now.

After school I waited to hear all about the Court Case Thing but at first no-one had anything to say about it. The grown ups all looked very smart but all they did was ask us about our day.

"Did you have a good day at school? Did you have a spelling test Laura-Louise? Did you play football on the field Andrew?"

When the polite small-talk fizzled out Andrew eventually asked about *their* day. The court case was all over very quickly, they said. Our father had not turned up. We would go on living where we were. That was it.

It was a relief really. 'Better the devil you know . . . .' some say. Our future had been determined for us by some strangers in high and mighty places. They had never seen me; didn't even know me. I had never smiled at them or offered them a sweet. I made up my mind to get on with the business of pleasing the people around me. Then they would love me.

Andrew had other important matters on his mind, mostly football and television. He was and still is an enthusiastic Liverpool supporter. He longed to go to Anfield to watch his heroes play live. They were doing well that season and Andrew likes a winner. Winning has always been important to him. He loves to *win.* He admires the great sportsmen and I give him credit for loyalty. Liverpool F.C.; Steve Davis; Michael Schumacher,—all the great winners of his youth. He supports them all. Grandma says that he is like his father. After the Court Case, Andrew just slipped back into the routine of life with our foster family. It seemed to him that the decision about our future was no big deal. It was not so easy for me. I tried to please everyone. I said what I thought people wanted to hear. I gave them presents, loving greeting cards that I had made myself with great care.

We didn't hear any news from our father for months. It was December and I was genuinely excited at the prospect of Christmas. Andrew and I got out the tall, silver Christmas tree that was Mother's. She had put it up last year in our lovely old house. It had been the first tree to go up in our street,—really, really early. It was as though she knew this would be her last Christmas and she wanted it to last for ever. I remembered helping her decorate it. This year was so different. In silence Andrew and I hung the baubles on the thin, tinsel branches. We thought of our mother and didn't need to speak.

All the usual preparations for Christmas were in full swing. There were school plays and parties and the end of term carol service. I sang a solo 'Away in a Manger' and a lady in the audience cried. It made me want to cry too. It was my mother's favourite carol. Pictures on cards of a young, serene Virgin Mary mothering her own baby Jesus made my grieving for my own mother even more poignant. I was excited about Christmas but I still missed her terribly and wanted her to be there to share the celebrations. My friends at school had all made special cards for their mothers. I didn't want to make one at all but the teacher said I had to because it was '***part of the curriculum***'. I could give it to my foster mother.

At church we were rehearsing carols too. All four children in our family were in the children's choir. We were going to go out carol-singing. Then, suddenly, out-of-the-blue

31

came a telephone call from our Real Dad. Mum answered the 'phone. I knew it was him straight away. He had a strong, powerful voice and I could hear him. Mum was tense. I stood very close trying to hear what was being said. I watched and waited, thinking I would soon speak to him.

"I'm sorry," Mum said on the 'phone, "The children are all going out carol-singing tonight. They've been rehearsing for ages. It is not convenient but we could . . . ."

My father's voice got louder interrupting her.

"Are you stopping me seeing my own children?" He sounded cross and I thought he had been drinking. I remembered what that sounded like. Mum tried to answer him. I stood close listening. The voice stopped abruptly. There was silence. Mum put the 'phone down. Then she turned on me.

"That was very rude of you to stand there listening to adults' conversations."

"But it was **_my_** father. I wanted to speak to him. I haven't spoken to him for ages." I pleaded in vain.

We all went carol-singing. I sang:

'Round yon virgin, mother and child' but I wasn't thinking of baby Jesus.

A few days later Mum and Dad had a long letter from our father. He was complaining that he had not been allowed to see his children and had contacted his solicitor. A lady came to talk about it. She visited us sometimes. She was nice. She always had time to talk to Andrew and me. Once, she helped me with my homework. I know now that she was a Social Worker monitoring the fostering arrangement but then I saw her as a friendly visitor who had time to listen to me. On this occasion she had a lot to say about the Carol

Singing incident. I didn't know what to tell her. I didn't want to say anything against my Real Dad and it was in my best interests to remain loyal to Mum and Dad. I wanted to please everyone. What did she want me to say? I just shrugged, pouted and offered her one of my sweets. I ran upstairs. I had a secret. I looked in my school coat pocket. I had a small scrap of paper with a telephone number written on it. My father had given it to me the day we went to the hairdresser's. It was his home number. No one knew I had it. Not even Andrew.

"You 'phone me whenever you want to." he'd said. I felt it needed to be a secret and there was never an opportunity to use the 'phone without everyone in the house knowing it. I'd have to wait for the right moment. I studied the number, saying it over and over in my head, committing it to memory before poking it back into my coat pocket.

My chance came a few days later when Mum went to the corner shop and everyone else was busy. I crept guiltily to the telephone and dialled the number I had memorised. My father's gruff voice answered abruptly.

"Hello. Who is it?"

"It's me." I whispered nervously.

"Who's that? Speak up. I can't hear you." I thought he sounded cross

"It's me. Laura. You said I could 'phone you."

His manner melted into sweetness.

"Hello Precious. What's the matter?"

"Hello." Suddenly, I didn't know what to say.

"What's the matter Sweetheart?"

"I'd like to see you again."

"I'd like to see you too Sweetheart but it's not easy. I

wanted to see you at Christmas and give you a present but *they* wouldn't let me."

"Mum made me go Carol-Singing."

"Don't you dare call her 'Mum'." he nearly exploded. "She's not your Mum. Don't ever, *ever* call her that again. Remember?"

"I gotta go. Bye!" Hurriedly, I put down the 'phone as she came back from the shop.

"Hello Mum!" I called. "Would you like a cup of tea? I'll put the kettle on for you."

"Thank you Love. What a good girl you are Laura-Louise."

I smiled. That was just what I wanted her to say.

NOCTURNE

"Laura-Louise! Laura-Louise!" My Mother's young voice called me through the mist. I heard her. I wanted to see her.

My eyes scanned the dimness, looking for the horizon but there was none. Only mist.

I scratched at my eyes to see more clearly. Everything was grey.

The greys gathered together and I watched the sun setting and rising again in perpetual motion. Gold rings of light gave the idea of horizon.

"Laura-Louise! Laura-Louise! Tea's ready!"

The mists were clearing and I became aware of the swirling bubbles of pain in my ears. I wanted to hear her voice more clearly. I clawed and scratched frantically at my ears till blood flowed clear and red, colouring the mist like a beautiful sunset. Her voice was fading fast.

Gold, finless fish floated airily towards me through the clouds; a whole shoal of them moving together, synchronised like a perfectly choreographed ballet. They were all around me; above, below, to front and back. I was falling, floating, flying. I reached out to touch the golden fish but felt only the icy mist. It seeped through my fat fingers.

Her voice had gone. I tried to listen but there was no one there. Nothing now. My ears ached and the only sound was that of my own heart beating and my own steady breathing breaking the ache of silence.

Incongruous music like that of distant country dancers began,—faintly, almost imperceptibly at first then louder and closer. I could see them now; a formation of frenetic

35

dancers dressed in black and white, their feet not touching the ground. A solo voice was singing so crisp and clear. Her notes pierced the clouds. She sung familiar words.

> *"You are my sunshine . . .*
> *My only sunshine.*
> *You make me happy when skies are grey."*

I knew that song. I knew that voice. My Mother was singing to me again, just like she did when I was a baby. It was just for me. But the grey skies were gathering again and blotting out her voice.

"You'll never know dear . . . ." Then echoing:

"You'll never know dear . . . . Y o u 'l l n e v e r k n o w d e a r . . . ."

CHAPTER 6

Most of my friends lived the school days waiting for the weekend. I began to live the weekend waiting for the familiar old security of the school timetable.

Despite my desire to please, my school reports were not good. As my work deteriorated so Andrew's work seemed to improve—and I had been labelled 'the bright one.'

As Winter melted into Spring, yellow flowers bloomed in the garden and Easter eggs appeared in the shops. I was reminded of my mother. The last time I had visited her in hospital I had taken her a bunch of those yellow, trumpety flowers and she had given me a huge, chocolate Easter egg. These are the things that still remind me of her last days.

Heavy rain caused rivers of dirty water to run down the gutters. It was the anniversary of her death and although the date didn't mean anything that year there were lots of things to force me to think of her.

Life seemed to go on and Katy and I were booked to go away on a residential holiday with the Brownies. Mum helped us to pack our suitcases with warm clothes and sun-hat, with plates and mugs, teddy bears and notebooks and pencils. I ticked things off the list as we packed.

"Everything but the kitchen sink!" Mum laughed.

She came to see us off. We all looked so smart in our Brownie uniforms as we climbed aboard the coach. I was excited. I sat next to Brown Owl and held her hand. Mum stood and waved. We all waved and shouted as the coach pulled away. I could see Mum smiling and waving and suddenly it crossed my mind that she had a whole week at home without me and maybe she was happy about it. Why else would she be smiling?

"You all right Love?" asked Brown Owl.

"Mmm." I tried to smile.

I turned to see Katy chatting to her friends.

The holiday with the Brownies was fun. There was so much to do from morning to night. I made lots of new friends but mostly I stayed with the grown-ups. I helped them to prepare the meals, wash up and tidy. On our last evening Brown Owl presented lots of badges and prizes and certificates. She announced that there was a special prize for a very special Brownie. We all wondered who it was.

"Someone," she said, "who had been the happiest and most helpful Brownie all week." Then she said the name. "Laura-Louise!"

It was me! It was really me! I stepped forward and took my certificate and my prize,—a fluffy, toy rabbit. I named him Brownie and I felt very proud.

We travelled home on the coach and Mum was there to meet us. The sun was shining. I hardly recognised her. She had had her hair cut very short and was wearing a new Summer dress. Coming back to familiar streets and shops I felt as though I had been away ages. Mum kissed me first and then Katy. I think she was pleased to see us. I told her all about my certificate and special prize. Katy was quiet. I showed Mum the toy rabbit.

"His name is Brownie!" I explained.

"That's funny," she said, "because we have a special present for you at home too."

"Just for me?

"For everyone." Mum replied.

"What is it? What is it?" I was too excited.

"Wait and see." she said mysteriously.

When we got home Mum took us to the garden shed. Whatever could it be?

Inside was a wooden hutch and in that was the cutest brown and cream Dutch rabbit,—a real, live one with a twitchy nose. I looked at Mum. I looked at the rabbit. Mum smiled. The rabbit went on twitching his nose.

"Is he mine?" I asked hopefully. The other children gathered round.

"What do you want to call him?"

"Oh! He's sweet! He needs a sweet name."

"What about 'Honey'?"

"Can I hold him?" Mum lifted the rabbit gently out of his hutch. I held him and stroked his soft fur. "I think I'll call him 'Fudge' because Andrew likes fudge."

So that was it. Fudge became part of the family. I loved him and made a fuss of him. I talked to him when I needed someone. The other children shared him but I was in charge of looking after him. Looking back, I think that Fudge did a lot to make me feel 'at home.'

"Can I make some fudge?" asked Andrew one morning after breakfast.

"Maybe later." replied Mum looking at the clock.

"Can I have a pet snake?" he persisted. "I'd like a big snake, a Burmese Python. I'd look after it. Laura Louise looks after Fudge."

"No! You can't have a pet snake." Mum sounded adamant.

"I'd feed it myself."

"That's what I'm afraid of!" laughed Dad. "That you'd feed it ***yourself***."

Grown-ups say stupid things sometimes. Andrew didn't think it was funny.

We already had a little white cat that I loved. The vet. had said that she was too fat and needed to go on a diet. Mum kept the cat food in the cupboard but she still mewed for more. I loved it when she rubbed round my legs. Sometimes I would creep out to the kitchen and open a new tin of cat food to feed her. One day I got into trouble for that. Mum looked in the cupboard.

"Where's all the cat food gone?" she demanded. "I know there was more here."

I kept quiet. The cat rubbed round my legs. Mum fussed around the kitchen. Then she found the empty tin in the rubbish.

"Do you know something about this?"

"No-oo." I lied.

"Well the cat didn't open the tin herself."

I laughed. "Perhaps Katy did it. She does sometimes." I hesitated. I knew I was in trouble but I was only trying to help. I put the kettle on. "Shall I make you a cup of tea?" I asked, trying to wriggle out of it.

I still got into trouble.

CHAPTER 7

"I got second prize! I got second prize!" I shouted as we burst in the door home from the fancy dress party. Katy and I were excited. It had been a brilliant fun party with our friends.

"Look Mum!" I chatted on. "I got a prize!" Everyone liked my green witch costume. My face, neck, arms and legs were all painted green. I knew I looked very scary.

"Well done!" encouraged Mum. "Now upstairs in the bath to wash off all that green stuff."

I took one more look at myself in the mirror.

"Woo . . . oooh!" I made a scary witch noise.

"Chase you upstairs!" said Mum and I ran on ahead pretending to be scared. I took my prize with me and put it beside my bed. Katy was quiet. She was often quiet these days. I had a lot to say. I sat thoughtfully in the bath of green, soapy water, letting the warmth envelop me. I felt safe, comfortable and . . . . happy. Yes I was happy.

Katy was in the bedroom getting changed out of her skinny skeleton costume.

"I got second prize!" I called out again from the bathroom to no-one in particular.

Mum was in the bedroom helping Katy change. I could hear them talking.

"Isn't it good that Laura-Louise won second prize. How did you get on Darling?"

I heard Katy's quiet reply.

"I won first prize. Look Mum!"

I slid down under the warm, green foam, right down. I didn't want to hear. I had got second prize but I hadn't told anyone that Katy had won first prize.

Breaking up from school at the end of the Summer term was a mixture of emotions. I would miss my friends and my teacher and my favourite dinner-lady who always gave me sweets. But those long, sunny, Summer days seemed to stretch out ahead into a future of eternity. No school for six whole weeks!

We were all going to Cornwall to see Grandma. I would be such a joy to see her again. I knew she loved me. The train journey from Paddington lasted all day but we had games to play and books to read. I could never concentrate for long reading a book especially on a train, there were too many other things going on.

"Are we nearly there yet?" asked Andrew for the millionth time.

"Shut up!" snapped David.

An argument ensued between the two boys.

Mum said, "Don't say Shut-up!"

Dad said "Come on David sit on my lap and look out of the window. We'll see the sea soon."

I climbed surreptitiously onto Mum's lap. Katy put her thumb in her mouth and curled up in the corner with her eyes closed.

I whispered in Mum's ear, "She's older than me and she still sucks her thumb." Mum pushed me off her lap.

"It's too hot for laps." she said. I looked across at David still on Dad's lap.

"Are we nearly there *now*?" asked Andrew again. "We're near the sea."

No-one answered.

Grandma was waiting for us at Penzance station. When she saw us all her face stretched into a big, wrinkly smile. She hugged me first then everyone else in turn. Even Mum and Dad got a hug. The smell of fennel tea filled my nostrils once more. It's a smell that will always transport me back to those childhood days with Grandma.

"You smell nice Grandma!" I said as I took her hand and we walked to the big taxi.

The holiday was just what a holiday should be. Long, hot sunny days on the beach, swimming and jumping over the waves, exploring rock pools. Andrew loved the beach. He has dark auburn hair and freckles. Mum was always slurping sun-tan lotion on him and telling him to keep his T shirt on or he's burn, even in the sea.

One day when we had all been for a swim, Mum made him put on his shirt and trousers. He was cross and stomped off across the rocks. A few minutes later we heard a yell. Mum and Dad stood up quick to look as Andrew came walking back dripping wet and sobbing.

"I fell in a big rock pool." he wailed.

He dried out pretty quickly in the sun but after that we always took a complete set of spare clothes for Andrew. Grandma named it the 'Rock-Pool-Special. After swimming everyone else seemed to dry quickly on the beach but my long, thick, dark hair took hours to dry. Katy's hair was long too but fine and fair. It dried quickly. My hair is not a bit like that.

On the way back from the beach we went to meet

Grandma from work. She had a clever job in a lovely office. She showed us round and introduced us to all her colleagues. Four sandy, weary children traipsed through smart offices being shown off. At each introduction Grandma said:

". . . . and this is Laura-Louise. Look at her straggly, wet hair!"

I just got more and more embarrassed.

"Tomorrow," Grandma promised, "I will take you out shopping and buy you a swimming hat."

My heart sank. No-one wears swimming hats these days. She went on;

"I can't have you wandering around my offices with wet hair dripping over all the important papers."

So, true to her word she took me into the big chemist shop in Penzance where there was a vast display in the window of flowery, colourful swimming hats. She made me try lots of them on,—in the shop—with people watching.

"Well, which one do you like?" she asked. I remained silent. "Well come on, say something."

I grunted.

"Well, if that's your attitude, I'll choose one for you." She chose a green hat with pink and yellow plastic flowers all over it. It was very expensive. I never did wear it.

Mum hired a car while we were in Cornwall, a green Cortina and she drove us to theme parks and zoos and gardens and museums. We found secluded sandy bays where we were the only ones on the beach. I was happy, immensely happy. I didn't miss school and my friends one bit. Grandma's house was cosy and comfortable. She always asked us what we liked to eat and I got some of favourite meals. Andrew liked Chille con Carne. I like salad and banana custard. It was all too good. I waited for the bubble to burst.

It was our last night and as I lay in bed I could hear Andrew moaning and crying quietly. I heard him get up and go in to Mum and Dad. Grandma got up too. They were all on the landing.

"My legs hurt!" he moaned.

"It's sun burn." said Mum. "Take your pyjamas off and then they wont rub. You'll feel cooler then."

"No fear! I ain't gonna bed naked!" huffed Andrew.

"I ah '***am not***' going to bed naked." corrected Grandma in a posh voice.

"I'm . . . *ah* . . . not going to bed . . . *ah* . . . naked." mimicked Andrew.

There was silence for a moment then everyone laughed so I got up too. I didn't want to miss anything.

"Please can I have a drink of water?" I asked. Mum went to the fridge to get some chilled drink. Grandma exclaimed;

"I know what Andrew could wear in bed!" and she ran to the airing cupboard. She returned holding up a massive pair of men's baggy underpants that had once belonged to Long-Deceased Grandad. Andrew hid in the bathroom to put them on and returned with a big smile.

"These are just right. I'll wear these."

And so he did and we all went back to bed.

CHAPTER 8

After the holiday we returned to the familiar routine of school and church and family life. I heard from Robbie and Jenny but we didn't hear anything from Real Dad . . . not even at Christmas. I guessed he was cross with me. I still had his telephone number but didn't dare call him. Perhaps he didn't want me like he used to. If he was really mad at me it would spoil everything and I was working so hard at being accepted by my foster family.

"Do you like going to Brownies?" asked my friend's Mum one day.

"No! It's horrible." I lied, "But **they** make me go."

"Oh you poor dear!" She hugged me and I smiled.

Another birthday came around and plans for celebrations but still there was no word from Real Dad. I knew I must have done something wrong. I tried another secret 'phone call but there was only a strange buzzing sound on the line; no ringing sound, no friendly voice. I put the 'phone down hastily.

Easter time and the daffodils and chocolate eggs reminded me of the last time I saw my Mother at the hospital. My memories of her were fading. Sometimes I closed my eyes and tried to picture her face, but she always appeared pale and tired. It made me sad. I was just beginning to feel a part of this family now and all the other relations of our extended family were good to me. Granny Bridgeman came to stay. She was Mum's Mum so Katy and David's granny. She always brought presents for us, all of us, me too. I liked to sit on her soft lap. She had time to just sit and listen to me.

"Happy Easter!" I whispered in her ear and I popped a piece of my chocolate egg in her mouth.

"Thank you darling! Happy Easter to you too. Bless you!"

"We're all going to visit a big, old castle tomorrow." announced Mum. "It should be really good fun."

I thought it didn't sound much fun at all. Castles were like museums and you only visited them on school trips.

"Bor . . . ing!" moaned Andrew but Katy and David seemed excited.

"Will there be an Easter egg hunt in the big garden?" they asked.

"I expect so."

There was . . . . and it *was* fun. We all went, even Granny came. There were lots of people there. We wandered round the huge gardens, through the woods, round the lake looking for cream eggs. I stayed close to Granny. She looked after me when I climbed a tree. I searched everywhere but I never found any chocolate eggs. When I saw Andrew he had a big cheeky, chocolaty smile on his face.

"Hey! Guess what?" he called. "Guess what I found?"

"Did you find an egg?" I asked jealously.

"Better than that!" he replied. "I found the lady who was hiding them so I followed her. Look! I've got seventeen . . . . Aah . . . Well only eight now . . ."

"Trust you!"

He pulled some sticky tissues out of his pocket oozing with melted chocolate and cream. He licked it, pleased with himself.

"Can I have a bit?" I asked timidly. "I didn't find **any**."

"Here y'are!" He offered me the sticky gunge. I looked at it.

"Mmm. Thank you but maybe not after all. I might get chocolate on my coat and I don't want to get into trouble."

Mum, Dad, Katy and Granny joined us.

"Hey! Guess what I found?" bragged Andrew again and he told them and showed them the contents of his coat pocket.

"Lovely." said Granny unconvincingly.

"Where's David?" asked Mum. "I thought he was with you."

"I thought he was with *you*. I haven't seen him for ages." Nobody had.

Panic ensued. *Where's David?*

"You all stay here. Don't move." organised Dad. "He might come back here. I'll go looking for him."

The castle grounds were massive and there were thousands of people there.

Dad went off. We waited and waited. I saw the panic in Mum's face and heard the despair in Dad's voice echoing round the gardens calling and calling.

"David! David! Where are you?" His voice was fading into the distance.

"Can we go in the castle now?" I asked.

"Of course not." snapped Mum. "Not while David is missing. He's only six. We must stay here."

I heard Dad's voice in the distance. Still calling, panic increasing.

"David! David!" His voice squeaked. "David . . . . David . . . . DA-VID!!"

I began to think. Suppose, I wondered, . . . just suppose it had been me that had gone missing. Would they have gone looking for me? Would they have shown the same fear that I could see now? Did they feel the same about me as they did about Katy and David? I got my answer sooner than I expected.

Mum and Granny had got into conversation with another lady.

"How may children have you got?" she asked.

Mum replied promptly, "Four."

"But only two *real* ones." corrected Granny.

I gasped. Then silence . . . an awkward silence. The lady laughed. I moved away and went to sit with Andrew. He was still eating chocolate.

The search for David eventually ended when Dad went back to the car-park. Amidst the hundreds of cars, there was David was sitting contentedly on the bonnet of our car!

"I got lost!" he said calmly. "So I knew if the car was still here, you were all still here. A lady gave me a chocolate egg but I ate it."

Mum hugged him tearfully. "What a sensible boy you are! And you're only six."

We all went home but now I knew how they felt about me. I must try harder.

I want to be *Real.*

CHAPTER 9

"I want to see my children." Real Dad demanded on the telephone. I could hear his powerful voice.

"At last!" I thought. "Oh yes, at last!" I so wanted to see him again . . . to know that he wasn't mad at me. Mum was trying to explain something to him. I was jumping up and down with excitement but then tried to be patient. Surely she would let me speak to him. He was *my* Dad. Real Dad. What were they talking about?

"Yes," said Mum. "She's right here beside me. I'm sure she'd like to speak to you. I nodded so hard I jumped up and down again and my long hair flew over my eyes. She handed me the 'phone.

"Hello Dad. How are you? I said politely.

"Hello Sweetheart." He sounded just the same as ever. "I've missed you."

"I've missed you too."

"Sorry I haven't been in touch for a while. I've been away . . . . with the army . . . in another country. It's tough over there. They wouldn't let me write to you. But now I have moved to a big house. You could come and see me. Would you like that?"

"O yes please! Yes please!"

You could come and see me and Kirsten and *our* children. You'd like it here. We've got a big house in the country with a big garden and a swimming pool. There are horses in the field. I could come and fetch you."

"When?"

"Tomorrow."

"Tomorrow? But that's . . . . TOMORROW!"

He laughed. "I'll pick you up at ten o'clock. Bring your swimming things. Does Andrew want to speak to me?"

"He's upstairs. I'll call him."

Andrew was playing with his racing car set. He didn't seem to keen to interrupt his game to go and speak on the 'phone.

"But it's Real Dad!" I persisted.

Mum told him firmly. "Go and talk to your Dad Andrew. You must speak to him. You haven't heard from him for ages."

Andrew grunted. He grunted even more on the 'phone and I think Real Dad told him off about it. o0o

And so we spent the next day at his house. It was very strange seeing him again. I knew that I had changed but he had changed too. He was still very strong and suntanned but he'd grown a beard. It suited him but it was scratchy when he kissed me. He told us that he was in the Army now. It was a very special secret army.

"Do you want to see my gun?" he asked.

"Cor yeah!" enthused Andrew.

"Speak properly. You are picking up very bad habits."

He showed us his gun. It was very heavy. Andrew was clearly impressed.

"Have you ever killed anyone?" he asked matter-of-factly.

"I can't answer that." replied Dad secretively and he put the gun away.

It was a good, sunny day and I played in the paddling pool with the young children. I helped to look after them while Kirsten went shopping. We splashed and played until we got cold.

"It's chilly on the willy!" announced the littlest one. We all shrieked with laughter so he said it again. And again. And again. We all repeated it over and over.

"Chilly on the willy! Chilly on the willy!" We roared.

In the afternoon Kirsten washed my hair in the bath. She put lots of shampoo and some smelly conditioner on it and then spent ages combing it through. It took a lot of combing.

"Ouch!" I yelled as she tugged at a tangle.

"You really must look after your hair." She insisted. "*My* children go to a ***proper*** hairdresser every six weeks."

She got out some electric curling tongs and set my hair in long ringlets.

"You look beautiful now Darling." said Real Dad. I like to see my girls looking beautiful. Come and sit here by me. I need to talk to you. Where's Andrew?"

"He's down the garden talking to the ponies in the field."

"Then I'll tell you my news. It's just for you Sweetheart."

"What is it Daddy?" He looked serious.

"Well," he began; "As you can see Kirsten and I have this lovely big house now. The Aunts gave me some money to help pay for it. We have children of our own and maybe soon ***more*** children. But you, Sweetheart are mine too. I remember that you asked me once if you could come and live with me. I didn't have room then but I do now. The Aunts help me. I've got a job as a lorry driver."

I thought you were in the Army."

"Yes. I drive lorries in the Army but don't interrupt.

What I want to tell you is . . . You **can** come and live with me now. What do you say?"

I didn't know what to say. I opened my mouth like Grandma had said but couldn't think of any words to let out the muddle going round in my head.

He went on. "I will write a letter to Social Services and one to Grandma in Cornwall because she is your Legal Guardian. You must give me her address. Then you can come and live here. You could move in quite soon. You could have that little bedroom at the back. You can see the horses from there. There's a very good school near here. They wear grey blazers and the girls wear big grey hats. My children will go there when they are old enough. You'd like it there. It's very expensive. You'd get a good education."

I still remained silent. Then I found the words to express one big question that was going round in my head.

"What about Andrew?"

"I think he is happy living where he is. That is the best place for him. He can stay there. I want **you**." I was silent again. He stroked my hair.

"It's a big secret at the moment," he continued, "so don't tell that foster family. Don't tell anyone. It's our special secret. We have some special secrets don't we Sweetheart?" He touched my knee. I looked at him. He leaned forward and his beard scratched my face. I got up.

"O.K. Dad. I'll keep it a secret."

Before we left I gave him Grandma's address. I knew it well. I could recite it although I didn't know how to spell the strange Cornish words.

We were tired when we got home. I told everyone about our day. I told them about the paddling pool. I told them how we laughed when the littlest one said 'chilly on the willy.' David laughed so much he fell off his chair. "Chilly on the willy! Chilly on the willy!" he shrieked.

That night I lay in bed thinking. If I go to live with Real Dad, . . . **when** I go to live with Real Dad, I'll miss Andrew. He's always been there; the one constant factor in my short life. I'll miss my friends. I'll go to a new school and wear a grey hat and blazer. I began to cry.

It was hard keeping secrets.

NOCTURNE

"Laura-Louise! Laura-Louise!" My Mother's voice was weak. She called me again and again. I wanted to run to her. Where was she?

The white door before me was shut. I knocked timidly. I could still hear her calling. I tried to reach the handle but I was too small. The door began rattling, banging against its frame as though there were a hurricane on the other side. I stretched all my muscles in a supreme effort to reach that handle and open the door. When it yielded I fell forward, tumbling through the opening. I looked for my Mother.

"Laura-Louise! Laura-Louise!" She was still calling but all I saw in front of me was another door. I reached to open it and found door beyond door beyond door. Doors within doors. Doors after doors. Doors upon doors. White doors that banged and rattled in the wind deafening me. I put my hands over my ears. My head ached. I couldn't hear her voice any more. A grey carpet unrolled before me invitingly. I stepped cautiously. Step after step. Following, listening, stepping, hoping.

There appeared yet another door, bigger than any of the others. It was calm and still. Everything silent. No hurricane. No voice. Silence.

I stood looking up at the door. I saw locks and bolts, chains and bars but no handle. I felt in my pocket for the key.

There was only dust.

CHAPTER 10

"Turn that light off!" shouted Mum. "You keep leaving it on when there's no-one in the room. It costs money!" Mum nagged me again. 'Turn the light off! Shut the door! Hang up your coat! Tidy your room!' There was always something that I was doing wrong. Mother was not a bit like that. She had been beautiful and fun, never lost her temper, never told me off, always there with a reassuring smile.

I was still living with my foster family. Birthdays, Christmases and sunny holidays with Grandma in Cornwall came and went. I waited to hear from Real Dad but there was nothing. Every day I rushed to answer the 'phone, to be first to pick up the post but there was absolutely no news. I strengthened my determination to please *everyone*.

It was hard growing up. As I approached adolescence I was glad to have Katy as a sister and confidante. We were the same age. We talked about boys and sex, about God and politics. We discussed the changes in our bodies. It was scary yet exciting. One rainy afternoon we got out our dolls.

"You haven't played with your dolls for months." said Mum. We played a game then put them away. For ever.

I talked to Katy about the funny feelings I get in the mornings like flashes of light in the mirror and reflections in the plates and cups that bounced off my eyes. I didn't like it. It hurt my head. I tried to tell Mum.

"You're just growing up." she said dismissively. I didn't like this sort of growing up. Does everyone feel like this I wondered. I was sure it wasn't normal.

"The flashing sunlight through the trees hurts my eyes and reaches into my head." I explained. "I get these 'funny feelings' like I've been here before then I can't remember where I am."

The 'funny feelings' went on for months. Mum suggested that we went to see a doctor but we never did. I suppose 'funny feelings' is not a recognised medical symptom.

Then it happened. In a second it changed my life for ever. Mum and I were the only ones in the room. I was curled up in the soft armchair. We were watching 'Top of the Pops' on television. Flashing strobe lighting reached into my head. I hugged a cushion and screwed up my eyes. My body reacted and vibrated in a spasm of uncontrollable quivers and shivers. Then sense evaporated into oblivion. Someone shouted:

"Stop it! Stop it! *Now!*"

But I couldn't stop it. It had hold of me. It held me in its grasp and shook me like a terrier with a young rabbit.

When I 'awoke' I wondered why there was a doctor in the room.

"I'm fine." I said.

"You've had a fit." he explained.

"You've been unconscious for nearly an hour." added Mum.

I didn't know what they were saying. It was all Mumbo-Jumbo. Andrew came in. He looked at me. He looked scared.

"What's happened? What's happened?" he panicked.

"Laura-Louise has had a fit." said Mum calmly. "Those 'funny feelings' that we didn't understand must have been leading up to it." She turned to me. "I'm glad I was here with you when it happened. Do you think it could have happened before?" No-one knew the answer to that one.

"What did I do?" I asked. I wanted to know.

The doctor said that I needed to go to hospital.

"I don't like hospitals." I objected.

"Not right now. You won't have to stay there. Just go for an appointment in a few days time. You might never ever have another fit in your life but I'd like you to see a specialist. He will probably give you some pills to take."

"My Mother had to take pills." I said, but no-one took any notice. The doctor was talking to Mum.

CHAPTER 11

Epilepsy took over my life. There were hospital appointments and meetings and pills and days off school. I had more fits. I lived in fear of having a seizure and wondered what I did when I was fitting. Mum said I sometimes fell on the floor and banged my head. One day I fell down stairs and bit through my lip making a hole. One day I hit my head against the radiator and made it bleed. Once I fell when I was making a cup of tea and the boiling water scalded by arm and chest. Sometimes I had as many as five fits in a day. One rainy afternoon I got sent home from school. Everyone thought it was because I had had a fit.

It was worse than that. Now I had 'nits'.

I decided that the world would be a better place without me. I wanted to just melt away, disappear into thin air. Maybe I could do something that would take me to where my Mother is, somewhere up with the angels. Is she an angel? Is there a heaven? Will I ever get there? Maybe I am too bad to get to heaven. I must have done something very bad to deserve all this. There were times when I seriously considered taking my own life. I was fourteen and I didn't want to be here. I didn't want to be me. Who could I talk to? I remembered what Grandma used to say about opening my mouth to let others know what was going on inside my head. I couldn't do that. I didn't even know myself what was going on inside my head. There was no-one that would understand.

I prayed to God. I even wrote him letters but he didn't answer them. I had prayed that my dear Mother would get better but she didn't. Even God didn't understand me.

One night, laying awake in my bed listening to the traffic passing I thought of my Dad, my real Dad. I wondered if he ever drove his lorry near our house. Would he have come to see us if he was near? I wanted to be with him. I didn't know how to contact him. He would understand me. He loved me, he wanted me and we had a secret, a special secret. I asked God to show me a way to find him again. I sat up and switched on the light. I wrote on a piece of paper: *"Dear God,* I want to live with my Dad." I felt better for writing it down. What next I wondered? I got up and with a small piece of sticky tape I stuck the letter to the outside of my bedroom door. I had tried that before but nothing had happened. I went back to bed and slept well. In the morning I remembered the note on the door. I got up quietly, even guiltily and looked. The note had gone! I looked on the floor. Nothing. No note. No sticky tape. Maybe God had taken it after all. I would await his reply.

I didn't tell anyone about it and for few days nothing happened. Then the Social Worker came to visit us. She always had time to talk to me and Andrew. I told her about school and about my friends; I told her about Fudge the rabbit. I was still looking after him. I even told her about my fits. They were still bad. I asked what I did when I was fitting. I thought it sounded silly when I said that I wanted to see someone else have a fit but she didn't laugh. She seemed to understand. But I didn't tell her about the nits. That was too bad to talk about.

She asked me about my Dad. She said she had a note that I had written. Did I really want to go and live with him? I was quiet. I wasn't sure what to say. Lots of thoughts rushed through my head as I remembered girls in grey blazers and posh hats. I remembered the paddling pool in the garden and the little children laughing. I remembered the horse in the field eating all the apples and I remembered my Dad saying that he loved me. I hung my head.

"Yes." I whispered into my jumper.

"Are you sure about that?"

"Yes." I looked up. She was listening to me, really listening with her eyes as well as her ears.

"What about Andrew?"

"I don't know."

"Would you like me get in touch with your Dad and tell him that you would like to live with him?"

I was quiet again. I had prayed to God for a way of reaching my Dad. Was this an answer to my prayer? I didn't know.

"I don't know where he is?" I said.

"I think I can get in touch with him. I could tell him that you would just like to *see* him again. Would that be all right?"

"Mmm." I mumbled.

"Sure?"

"Yes." I needed to say more, to be really polite. "Yes . . . please . . . . I'd like that."

"I'll see what I can do. I will have to talk to your Foster

Mum and Dad and also to Andrew. I will come and see you again soon and let you know what's happening."

It was a long time. It was a long wait. Did anyone want me I wondered? I only wanted to be loved. My Mother loved me. Real Dad loved me. He said he did. I was special to him.

I walked down the garden to the shed to talk to the rabbit; my rabbit, well . . . . *our* rabbit really but I was the one in charge of him so he was sort-of mine. I looked in the hutch. He wasn't there! I searched under the hay in the corners but he was definitely not there.

"Where's Fudge?" I ran into the house screaming. "Where's Fudge? Who's got him? Who's taken Fudge out of his hutch?"

But no-one had him. I asked them all. I searched back in the garden. I looked under the bushes and behind the trees. I asked the neighbours. Mum wrote some notices and put them up on lamp-posts.

"Has anyone seen my rabbit?"

but days went by and there was no response. Fudge had disappeared. God had answered my prayer but he must have taken the rabbit as payment. We never did find out what had happened. I hope someone found him and looked after him and talked to him like I did. I missed him. If he had died, I could have buried him. I could have coped with that. I knew what dying meant. But the rabbit had just disappeared. That was the worst thing . . . not knowing what had happened to him. Dad made a joke about a rabbit called 'Houdini' but I didn't think it was funny. Andrew shouted: "***Now*** I can I have a Burmese python? ***Plea . . . . ease***!"

I went to my room and cried.

CHAPTER 12

Moving house is stressful, traumatic at any age. We didn't move far, just around the corner to a much bigger house. I could have a room all to myself. It was a big, rambling red-brick old place, covered in leafy creeper and it needed lots of work. Mum and Dad were busy painting and decorating. Builders came and went. There was a new roof, new electric wiring and a lovely new fitted kitchen. I liked my bedroom. It was good having a it all to myself. I had some privacy at last. It made me feel grown up. It had a big window looking out over the street. I stood there watching. A young man was parking a yellow sports car. As he got out I saw his lovely, shiny long hair. He looked up and saw me at the window. I waved and he waved back. It made me feel all tingly and excited inside. He was nice. I watched him go into a house. I would remember to look out for him again. I went to my new mirror and dressing table and sorted out all my make-up. There wasn't much. I put on lots of green eye-shadow, then blue, then pink. I drew thick black lines around my eyes with an old eye-liner and exaggerated my lashes with heavy mascara. I looked in the mirror again. I brushed my long, dark hair and thought of the young man with the yellow car. Then I thought of Real Dad. I had been so busy and excited about the new house that I had almost forgotten him. I ran downstairs to Mum.

"I need to buy some new make-up." I asked and added "Please." as an afterthought.

"Gosh!" she exclaimed when she looked at my face. "It looks as though you have quite enough make-up already!"

"And I need some special shampoo and hair spray too." I ignored her comment.

"That all sounds very expensive." she replied as she carried on polishing the old banisters. "We don't have much money now. It's cost a great deal to buy this house and do it all up. I have to think about Katy too. I expect she would like to have her own make-up and special shampoo but it would cost too much money. There is always a big bottle of family shampoo in the bathroom. It smells of nice apples. And what about the boys? I know they don't want ***make up***," she giggled, "but they would think it wasn't fair if I bought you special stuff. They would want something too."

"I don't like that old, cheapy shampoo stuff. It's horrible and it stinks! If I had a little more pocket money I could buy my own."

"We'll see." she said and continued to clean the stairs. It didn't sound too promising so I went up to my room and thought about it. I would mention it to the Social Worker next time she came. I looked in the mirror then went to the bathroom to wash my face.

Over the next few days I saw the young man with the yellow car several times. I began to know his routine. I watched for him out of the window but mostly I kept hidden behind the curtain so he couldn't see me. I wondered what his name was and where he worked. At night, in bed I thought about him a lot. I imagined myself with him, stroking his long hair, and him with me, touching me.

Then I thought about my Real Dad and I wondered what he would think.

The next time the Social Worker came to see us I was keen to speak to her. I was still on medication for my epilepsy but fits were frequent. I chatted and smiled and offered her a chocolate. I drew a picture of a rabbit for her and told her how my rabbit had disappeared. Someone must have taken him. I missed him. Then I asked her about make-up. I explained that I liked to wear eye-shadow and liner and mascara. There was some cream for teenage spots and I would like some really nice shampoo I had seen advertised on television. I knew it was expensive. I wanted to buy some but Mum wouldn't let me. I said that Mum didn't understand that I was growing up and these things were important. She thought that I was still a little girl but I was fourteen. The big, cheap family shampoo in the bathroom smelled of apples. It was horrible. She said she would speak to Mum about it. Then she had the news I was really waiting for . . . . She had spoken to my Real Dad! And more than that . . . he wanted to see me! I was ecstatic! Over the moon! I couldn't stop smiling. I bounced with delight.

"When? When can I see him?"

"He will telephone you soon and you can talk to him and arrange a day and time that is suitable for you both." she replied.

"Ooh! I can't wait!" I bounced up and down on my chair.

"That's a funny expression . . . 'I can't wait . . .' You will **have** to wait but I don't think it will be long. Do you think Andrew will want to see him too?"

"Don't know. He doesn't say much. He's fifteen now and

he'll be leaving school soon. It's funny. I can't imagine him going out to work. He likes computers. He wants to go to College and learn more about them."

I left the Social Worker and went up to my room. Andrew spoke to her and I heard them talking about computers and College again. I wondered what she was telling him about our Dad. I looked out of the window. It was almost time for the young man with the yellow car to come home from work. I ran down stairs to see the Social Worker leave from the front door. I waved to her. Then I spotted the yellow car. I walked out to the front gate and stood in the garden. He parked his car outside our house and got out.

"Hello." I smiled at him.

"O Hi!" he called as he locked his car door. "Have you just moved here?"

He walked towards me. I giggled.

"What's your name? he asked.

I giggled again, then mumbled "Laura-Louise"

"Well, I'll see you again. I hope."

He went into his house . . . . just five doors up the road. I watched him, then I ran indoors up to my room and checked my make-up again.

"Mum, *please* can I buy some new make-up? The Social Worker says I *need* some *and* I need some of that special cream for my spots."

"You haven't got spots!" she replied and carried on preparing the dinner.

"But you have got some news about your Dad." she continued. "That's exciting isn't it. He's going to telephone one day soon and then you can meet him again. It's been a long time. Andrew might go to meet him too but he doesn't seem too bothered. You know Andrew. He's just thinking about leaving school and going to work and earning some money."

That night I had so much to think about. I had spoken to the good-looking young man and also, better than that . . . . my **Real** Dad was going to telephone! That night I had a strange dream but when I awoke I couldn't remember it.

CHAPTER 13

I was up early the next morning. There was a scrappy note on the mat by the front door, just a piece of lined paper folded really small. It must have come through the letter box. I picked it up and wondered who it was for. Written on the outside it said:

> "To Lolly-Pop
> -I think that's what you said your name was."

I opened it. It was a note to me from the young man with the yellow car!

How did he think my name was Lolly-Pop? I had been too excited when I spoke to him I must have giggled too much. Now I giggled again, nervously as I read the note.

> Dear Lolly-Pop
>   I think you are very nice. I like your smile. I think you like my car. I see you peeping out of the window when I park it.
>   I am going into town on Saturday morning. Would you like to come for a ride in my car? We could go to town and have coffee in a shop. I hope you can come because I like you. Drop a letter in my door. It's number 63.
> Love from Nigel xxxx

"Nigel?" I thought. "*Nigel*!" I rolled the name around on my tongue. It's not a name I had thought about. He didn't look like a Nigel. But then what does a Nigel look like? I would get used to it. Maybe. Would I get the chance to 'get-used-to-it'?

But wow! I had a date! My first real date with a boy. There had been boys at the church youth club, boys at school. They were good friends. I liked them. One of them had even sent me a Valentine card. I visited them and they had come to our house for tea. They were boys who were friends . . . but not boy-friends.

Back in my bedroom, I hid the note under my pillow. It was still early. The house was quiet. I had to get ready for school. I went to the bathroom and turned on the taps. I looked in the mirror. The light bounced around the shiny walls and into my head. When I regained consciousness I was on the floor in a pool of warm, soapy water. I could smell apples and hear water running. There was knocking and a voice calling:

"Laura-Louise! Laura-Louise! Open the door! Open the door! There's been another flood!"

It was bad. One of the worst fits I'd had. I had hit my head again and what seemed worse, the taps had been left on as I washed my hair, the bathroom floor was flooded and the kitchen ceiling below had come down dropping white flakes of plaster into the porridge. Lumps of plaster fell onto the big scrub-top table and water went on dripping steadily. My head ached a bit but apart from that I was fine. The seizure was over. I dressed and was ready to go to school. Dad went off to work. Mum was upset. She said she couldn't possibly go to work and leave the house in a state like that. It was the new house too and they had done so much work painting and decorating and fitting the kitchen. I wasn't sure whether Mum was upset because the new kitchen looked a mess or because I had had a bad fit.

It wasn't until I got to school and started chatting to my friends that I remembered the note from the young man with the yellow car. This epilepsy was certainly affecting my memory. Or was it the drugs? I tried to remember the young man's name. What had he signed on the letter? Was it Neil? No! Nigel! That was it. Nigel! It was terrible that I couldn't remember things properly. I couldn't even remember where I had put the note. He had called me 'Lolly-Pop'! It was a funny name but I liked it coming from him. He could go on calling me Lolly-Pop for ever! "For ever?" Why was I thinking in terms of 'for ever'? He had only just asked me out and we were going in his car to the town for a coffee in a shop. Then I remembered something else. I hadn't replied to his note! Would he think I wasn't interested? No he would be at work. I could write a letter to him as soon as I got home from school. I talked to all my friends about him. I told them about his long hair and his yellow car and his house. I told then about the lovely note he had written. They all laughed when I said he thought my name was 'Lolly-Pop'! They started to call me that name too. I liked it and I told them I was going out with him and he was my boy friend and he had a good job with lots of money. Then they told me to shut-up about him. I had gone on too long. I never did tell them about my fit and the flood in the bathroom and the kitchen ceiling falling down. I didn't invite anyone back to my house that day either. I had other things to think about.

Up in my bedroom, I took the note out from under

my pillow and read it again slowly. I had a date! I needed to write a reply. Whatever could I say? I scribbled a quick letter then ripped it up and threw it in the bin. I tried again. I wanted to let him know I liked him. I liked his yellow car but I preferred its driver! I wrote about four replies until I was fairly happy with one.

> Dear Nigel,
>   Thank you for your letter. My name is really Laura-Louise but you can call me 'Lolly-Pop'. I would like to come out with you to the town on Saturday morning. Thank you for asking me. I will look forward to it.
> Best wishes, Laura-Louise x (Lolly-Pop!)

I read it again. The 'best wishes' bit was an inspiration. It was better than mere '*from*' that was too formal and '*love*' was too forward. I drew a picture of a rabbit on it. I needed an envelope. I went to ask Mum. She was in the kitchen amidst the remains of the flood and the collapsed ceiling. I asked her for an envelope and she told me where they were. I took one and then took another two just in case I might need to write to him again. I delivered the letter to number 63 just before I knew he was due home. I watched from behind the curtain in my room until I saw the yellow car come round the corner then I ran to the kitchen.

"I'm really sorry Mum about the ceiling. I couldn't help it."

She gave me a hug.

CHAPTER 14

I was in love! I was fourteen and I was in love! The date with Nigel was great. I had spent ages deciding what to wear eventually settling for casual jeans and a smart pink top and a brown jacket. I spent so much time doing my makeup that I was nearly late. I told Mum that I was meeting 'a friend'. We went to the town in his car. He was a good driver. He told me about the road signs and asked me if I knew what they meant. It was a silly conversation for a first date. We went for a coffee in a shop. We talked about all sorts of things and I told him that I was fostered because my Mum had died when I was six and I didn't see my Dad. He touched my hand across the table and looked into my eyes. I looked at his face. His big brown eyes were smiling yet he seemed sad. He seemed surprised when I told him that I was fourteen.

"Blimey!" he cried. "I thought you were sixteen or seventeen at least."

"Katy's my foster sister she's a bit older than me but we're in the same year at school."

"Blimey!" he said again. "I thought she was younger than you. She's pretty and has lovely long, blond hair. I've seen her on her way to school."

I was concerned for a moment that he had noticed so much about Katy. I was already jealous of her willowy figure and looks. Nigel saw my face fall.

"But you look older and wiser and I like your dark hair."

He stroked my hair. I giggled.

"I like your long hair too." I said.

"My Mum hates it." he laughed. "She's always moaning at me to get it cut. I have to tie it back at work."

"Where do you work?" I asked.

"I drive a fork-lift truck in a warehouse. It's not much of a job but I get on well with my mates there. I'll never earn much money. I don't have any exams. or anything."

"I think it sounds a good job. Lots of people are unemployed these days. You're lucky to have work."

"One day I'll be rich. I'll be a millionaire! Well, we can all dream can't we!" He laughed. I laughed with him. I was beginning to like him more and more. He touched my hand. On the way back to the car we held hands and he asked if he could see me again.

I asked my friends at school,

"How can you tell after the first date if a boy really likes you?"

"You've got another date? He likes you!" they replied. I smiled.

I smiled a lot that day . . . in fact I smiled all that week.

I saw Nigel everyday after that. I watched him out of the window as he parked his car and he always waved. I rushed down stairs and we chatted over the garden wall. Mum asked me about him.

"He's nice." I said. "He makes me smile."

"I can see that." she grinned. "You haven't stopped smiling all week. Tell me about him."

I wanted to talk about him and yet I wanted him to be a bit of a secret. Telling Mum made our friendship somehow 'official.' A few days later I overheard her chatting in the 'phone.

". . . and guess what?" she said knowingly. "Laura-Louise has got a boy friend! She's totally smitten with him. He's a bit scruffy with jeans and long hair. He takes her out in his car and they had a coffee in town." I hadn't told her that last bit so I wondered how she knew. Was it just women's gossip? Of course, My Mum knew his Mum. They must have got talking too.

The next time I saw Nigel I asked him;

"Does your Mum talk to my Mum? Do you think they talk about us?" (Gosh! I'd said *'us'*. That made it sound as though we were a couple.)

"I dunno." He shrugged. "Do you want to go for a coffee in town again on Saturday? I need to be back to watch the football though. Chelsea are playing this week."

"Yes. Ok. I like to. Please. I could sit and watch the football with you too."

"Aah. You wouldn't want to do that. My mate Mark is coming round to watch the match."

"Does he know about me?"

"Yeah! I told him all about you. He wants to know if you've got a sister."

"Did you tell him about Katy?"

"Yes. I told him she's really pretty but she's only a little girl."

"She's taller than me. And she's older than me."

"Oh yeah! I forgot that. But you are more . . . er . . . more . . . I can't think of the right word."

"More what?"

"More . . . er sexy!" He smiled at me. I giggled. Then

he leaned forward, took my hand and kissed me gently on the cheek.

"Did you like that? he asked.

I was exhilarated! "Mmm." was all I could reply.

"There's plenty more where that came from! I'll see you Saturday! Bye!" He had gone. I watched him walk up to road to his house. I could see his Mum looking out for him. Perhaps she had been watching us. I went indoors.

Katy was doing her homework. Books were spread out across the dining table. I sat down silently and joined her. I tried to do my science homework. It was about 'osmosis' but I couldn't concentrate. Katy tried to help.

"I've done mine." she bragged confidently.

"I can't be bothered." I shrugged, pushed the books away and went upstairs to my room. I wrote in my diary. 'Today Nigel kissed me.' I didn't need to write anything else. Nothing else mattered. I lay on my bed and thought about him.

CHAPTER 15

The relationship with Nigel went well until one day I had a fit while I was out with him in a busy main shopping street. I was desperately embarrassed. I had told him about my fits and he had sounded sympathetic but I had dreaded it happening while I was with him. I didn't really know what I did while I was fitting. Did I show my underwear? How bad could it be? Did I make funny noises? What did he do? Some passers by came over to help. Nigel just stood there. He had never seen anyone have a fit before. Later, when we were seated in our usual cafe, he told me that he had wanted to help, to stop the fit but didn't know what to do. I explained to him that there was nothing anyone could do to stop the fit, just see that I didn't bump my head or hurt myself, then let the fit subside in its own time. He held my hand and said that if it ever happened again he would be there for me.

"Lolly-pop," he said, "I would do anything for you. You have become very special to me; very special indeed." Then he kissed me again. I responded in a way I had never known before. My Mother kissed me when I was little. My Real Dad had kissed me and told me I was special. We had a secret. My foster parents kissed me every night at bedtime, but that kiss from Nigel was a real, passionate kiss that awoke new feelings of excitement within me. He leaned close to me and I wanted to lean against him.

Oh, I knew the facts of life. I knew about the 'birds and

the bees' as Mum called it. She had talked to me about sex and growing up. We'd even had lessons about it in school. I knew I was growing up and I had chatted to my friends at school and we had giggled about periods and bras and boys but that kiss from Nigel on that day in that little cafe was my realisation of grown up feelings that I wanted to explore.

We walked home that day. He didn't have his car but that gave us longer to talk. I tried to explain about my fits and asked him what I did. He was kind. He told me how I stopped talking and shook my head and hands then fell to the floor in a trembling heap of lashing arms and legs.

What I really wanted to know was—did he see my pants? It was a silly thing but that was what bothered me most. I didn't like to ask him and he didn't say. When we got to my house I invited him in.

"I've got a new radio." I said. "Would you like to see it? We could listen to some music."

He hesitated and for a moment I thought I must have said something wrong. Then he smiled.

"Oh, er . . . . yeah . . . please. Would it be all right with your Mum? I mean . . . er . . . um . . . Mary . . . Do you call her Mum?"

"Oh yes." I replied. "Yes. I do call her Mum. It would be fine. I'm always allowed to bring friends home anytime. You are my friend aren't you?"

"I hope I'm more than just a friend now. We've been seeing each other for three weeks."

"Three weeks two days and . . ." I looked at my watch. "and three and a half hours!" We both laughed. I got out my door key and we went in.

"Hi Mum!" I called. "I've brought my friend Nigel round. Can I make him a cup of tea?"

Mum came running out from the kitchen drying her hands hastily on a tea towel.

"Nigel!" She beamed. "How lovely to see you! I've heard *all* about you." I knew that that last bit was not at all true. Mum had definitely not heard '*all*'. In fact she had heard very little about him. He looked worried. Mum shook his hand. I don't think he was used to shaking hands.

"Sorry!" apologised Mum. "My hands are still wet. You two go and sit in the lounge. Katy's in there watching something on television. I'll make the tea. Sugar Nigel?"

Poor Nigel looked nervous. We went to join Katy. She was lying on her belly on the floor, head propped up on her hands. She hardly took her eyes off the screen as we entered.

"Hi." she murmured.

We sat together on the sofa. He took my hand and stroked it gently. I wondered if Katy had noticed. I pulled away.

"I need to see Mum in the kitchen." I said. "Won't be a minute."

I told her that I had had another fit. She had to keep a record of my seizures for the hospital to monitor my medication. I told her how kind Nigel had been.

"He's really thoughtful Mum . . . and I really like him."

"I can see that!" She smiled knowingly." Here's your teas and help yourselves to biscuits."

"Thanks Mum!" I gave her a quick kiss on the cheek.

"Look out dear! You'll spill the teas."

After Nigel had gone home Mum came in, turned off the television and sat down beside me.

"I need to talk to you." she said seriously.

"Oh no!" I thought. "Not another talk about the 'birds and the bees'".

"Did you know that Nigel used to have another girlfriend? He went out with her for over a year. They had a flat together. He was mad about her."

I shrugged nonchalantly. I didn't want to listen. I didn't look at her.

"Did you know about her?" Mum asked.

"Yeah!" I lied.

"That's O.K. then. I just wanted to make sure you knew. His Mum told me all about her. They planned to get married and then she dumped him and she's now going around with someone else. He was terribly upset. I just thought you needed to know."

"Yeah." I said again and went upstairs to my room and buried my face in the pillow.

CHAPTER 16

You should never ask your partner about their previous relationships. I know that now. I learned the hard way. Nigel did tell me eventually about his last girlfriend but he said he liked me better.

"Come on Lolly-Pop!" he encouraged. "You know it's always best to have a bloke with experience . . . . and I could teach you a thing or two about men!" He pressed up against me. I leaned towards him and kissed him gently on the cheek. We embraced and kissed for a long time.

Our relationship grew and we saw each other regularly. We spoke every day when he got home from work. I would be looking out of the window at twenty past five, waiting excitedly. He still parked his yellow car outside our house and I would run out to see him. He was kind and thoughtful and he made me laugh. He began to recognise the early signs when I was going to have a fit and he would talk me through it, sit me down until the seizure began to ease. One day I realised that I had gone for a whole week without a fit. I went to the kitchen to talk to Mum about it. She was busy peeling potatoes.

"I didn't like to say anything yet." she replied. "You have been so much better. You seem calmer and happier too. I think Nigel is good for you."

"He's really good to me Mum. He knows when I am going to have a fit and he can talk me out of it."

"You've been seeing a lot of him lately and I know you

like him but remember you are still at school. You have exams. to work for. You are getting behind with your school work. Do you have any homework or revision to do now? I could help you with it."

"No." I snapped. "I don't have any homework. None at all. I'm seeing Nigel later and we're going to his friend's house. He says Katy can come too. She wants to come."

"What?!" shouted Mum vehemently. "You have asked *Katy* to join you? That was very deceitful of you Laura-Louise. It's not fair on Katy. She has been working so hard for her exams. She will do well. I don't want _her_ to throw away all her talent. She needs to stay in to revise. And yes, you _do_ have homework. I had a letter from the school to say that you were getting behind with your work. They want to know if there is anything wrong at home."

It was the first I had heard about the letter.

"There's nothing wrong!" I snapped. "You just said that you thought Nigel was good for me. Well, I am going to see him tonight. Katy can do what she likes." I stormed out and slammed the door behind me. The room shook. A bit of kitchen ceiling fell on to the old scrub-top table.

"Now look what you've done!" I heard her shout.

Katy and I did go out that evening. We went to Nigel's friend's house. We watched the football. Well, *they* watched the football. They had cans of beer. I sat next to Nigel on the big sofa. We cuddled up together. Mark sat next to Katy. He held her hand. I nudged Nigel.

"Look!" I whispered in his ear, "Look at Mark and Katy. They're holding hands."

"Blimey!" he replied, a little too loudly. "What'd your Mum think of that?"

"She'd go bananas!"

"I'd like to see your Mum go bananas!" he whispered jokingly and we both giggled.

Suddenly their team scored a goal. Mark jumped in the air nearly knocking Katy over. Nigel jumped and cheered too.

The game was over and I think their team won. They seemed pleased anyway. Nigel drove us both home.

"Did you have a good time?" I asked Katy when we got indoors.

"Yes, thank you. I had a lovely time" she replied politely.

"Did you get on well with Mark?"

"Yeah!" she giggled. "I'm seeing him again tomorrow. But please don't tell Mum. She'll go bananas." We both laughed.

And so for a few weeks at least we became a 'foursome'. We went out every Saturday evening sometimes visiting friends, sometimes to a cafe and sometimes to the pub.

One evening I sat in Andrew's bedroom. I had been so preoccupied with Nigel that I had not really taken much notice of my own dear brother. I needed to talk to him. He was growing up and would be leaving school soon.

"What will you do? Where will you go?" I asked.

"I'm going to college. I'm going to do a computer course. I like computers."

"But you haven't got a computer."

"No. Not yet. Mary and Len are going to buy me one." (I noticed he never called them Mum and Dad. To him they were always Mary and Len.)

"What?! You lucky beggar! I bet they'd never buy *me* anything as expensive as that."

"I dunno!" he shrugged. "It'll be *their* computer really so they will use it too but I can choose whichever one I want for my course."

"It's not fair!" I moaned. "I wish I had a computer. Can I use it sometimes too?"

"'Spect so!"

The Katy/ Mark relationship did not last long. He wrote her a very sexy letter. Mum found it. They stopped seeing each other after that. She decided to work hard at school for her exams. My relationship with Nigel seemed to be changing too. Was he getting bored with me I wondered? What should I do to please him? I bought him a book about cars. He told me he had never read a book in his life but he would treasure this one. I bought him a silver St. Christopher to wear round his neck. He wore it for a few days but I didn't see it again after that. I made a special card with a red satin heart. I even cut up my old red bra to make it. I wrote 'I LOVE YOU' inside. I didn't sign it. He would know who it was from. I dropped it through his door while he was at work. He never mentioned it. I didn't see him that Saturday. He and Mark were going to a football match. He said I wouldn't have enjoyed it anyway. He was probably right but I desperately wanted to be with him. More than that, I desperately wanted him to want to be with me. I feared our friendship was waning.

Christmas came and went. Mum and Dad organised a New-Year party. I invited Nigel but he didn't come. Valentine's Day I sent him a card but he never sent me one. A few days later I met his Mum walking past our house. She stopped and smiled and gave me a big hug.

"I'm so sorry, my dear. I hope you are not too

heart-broken. Are you coping?" I didn't know what she was talking about. She pushed me gently back and held me tightly and arms' length. She looked closely into my puzzled eyes.

"Oh, my dear, dear girl. You poor thing. You didn't know. He hasn't told you has he?"

I sniffed and listened.

"He has gone away my dear. He has gone back to his old girl friend. They have a flat together. Not far away. He should have told you. He really ***should*** have told you." She hugged me again and then went on her way.

CHAPTER 17

I had hardly noticed that Andrew was growing up too. He had left school and started the computer course but I could tell he was not enjoying it. It was much harder than he'd thought and not at all what he'd expected. He had made some friends there and they spent every evening in the pub. I told him that I was worried about him. He was special to me. He was the only person who had always been in my life and I needed him. I began to join them regularly in the pub each evening. His friends were nice to me. One in particular always welcomed me and bought me a drink. His name was Paul. He was tall, good looking and always smartly dressed. He seemed to have plenty of money. I didn't have enough money to buy drinks for others. Andrew didn't have much money either. I wondered how he could afford to buy so many beers. He was drinking a lot. Too much. He was only seventeen and he was drunk most evenings. Mum and Dad were worried too. After a few drinks he would talk and talk and get angry. He chatted up girls in the pub but never had a real girlfriend. One evening I had stayed home to finish off some school work. I was trying to be more conscientious. Andrew went to pub as usual. He came home very late and very drunk. Mum shouted at him.

"You shouldn't be drinking at all. You are only seventeen!"

"Silly old woman!" he screamed." Don't you know everyone drinks these days?!"

He ran up stairs swearing but instead of going into his own room he went into David's room. He sat there on the floor and lit up a cigarette. Mum followed him. David was in bed.

"Get out of that room!" she shouted angrily. "Get out! We have just had this room decorated specially for David. You are much too drunk! Get out . . . and put out that cigarette!"

Defiantly he stubbed the cigarette out several times on the new carpet leaving a row of smouldering holes.

"How **dare** you behave like that? Get out!" I'd never heard Mum so angry. Andrew swore again, then got up and pushed Mum out of the way.

"Don't you dare push me. Don't you dare . . . ."

"I'll push whoever I like!"

With that, he seemed to pick Mum up like a feather. He was bigger than her now. And stronger. He dropped her clumsily and she bumped heavily down the stairs. She landed awkwardly and lay still for a few minutes. I had watched un-noticed from below. Andrew went to his room. I didn't know what to do. I waited to see if Mum would move. She was breathing heavily. I could hear her moans of pain. Slowly she got herself up and went to her room. Dad was nowhere to be seen. I think he ran a boys' club at the church. I went to bed.

The next morning Mum and Dad were both there at breakfast. Mum's face and arms were very bruised. We were all summoned to a 'family meeting.'

It was not often that all six of us would sit down together these days. There was an awkward silence and a mood of finality.

Mum spoke first. "I have had enough." she said quietly and firmly. "I cannot cope any more. You may have noticed that Dad and I are not getting on. I have made a decision. We cannot all stay together living in this house. There must be some changes. I am telephoning Social Services. I cannot cope." She began to sob uncontrollably.

And suddenly there *were* changes. Andrew left home. He packed a small bag with his belongings. He slipped away silently on his own. I didn't know where. A Social Worker came to collect me. I didn't know her. I packed my suitcase; the same one that I had brought with me when I had moved in with the family ten years previously. Now I was moving out and I had no idea where I was going. I was sixteen and alone in the world. I climbed into the back of the Social Worker's car. Mum was standing at the front door. She was crying. She came over to speak to me. Her swollen, bruised face pressed against the car window.

"Have you got anything to say to me?" she asked quietly.

I hesitated. "Er, . . . Bye!" I muttered but I didn't look at her. I hung my head. I felt bitter and hurt and misunderstood. What had I done wrong to deserve all this? Why had everyone I had ever known let me down again? I must learn to never, ever trust anyone again. The car pulled away. Tight-lipped, I didn't shed a tear and I didn't look back.

CHAPTER 18

The next year passed in some sort of hazy oblivion. I moved into a room in a hostel that I shared with three other young girls. I did my best to keep my room clean and tidy. I was forever cleaning up the kitchen after the others. I think I was the only one who ever put out the rubbish. If I left it, it remained until the bin was stinking and overflowing. I wiped down the surfaces and bought cleaning materials. No-one else did. I had a stubborn determination to survive. I didn't need anyone else. The only person I could trust was myself.

Sometimes I would lay in bed and think about my childhood. I thought about the time with my real mother. I knew she loved me. She was beautiful. I had her photograph stuck up on the wall over my bed. My memory of her was fading. I tried so hard to remember things. *'Didn't we have a lovely time the day we went to Bangor!'* Every time I hear that song I think of her singing it to me and rocking me on her lap. How different things would have been if she had stayed with me. I thought about the times with the foster family. I remembered the holidays with Grandma in Cornwall. I remembered the Brownies and Guide camps. I remembered my old friends from school. I remembered the games that Katy and I used to play with our dolls. I worried about Andrew. I didn't know where he had gone. I prayed that he would get in touch with me. I thought about God. I didn't go to church any more. I had met my other half-siblings.

Where were they now I wondered. I thought about Nigel. I missed him. He had made me smile and he made me feel good about myself. But then he let me down too.

I thought about my Dad too. He was my Real Dad. I hadn't seen or heard from him for years now. I wondered if he would want me now. Would he want me the way he used to want me? Would he touch me like he used to? I wasn't his 'pretty little girl' any more. I was grown up.

I was still on medication for epilepsy and my flat mates said it was affecting my memory. Sometimes I tried to remember; sometimes I didn't want to remember.

The Social Worker came to the flat to visit us all. I was chopping up onions and mushrooms for my dinner. Tearfully, I confided in her:

"If ever I have children of my own I shall make sure they have a really, really happy time."

"Would you like to have children?" she asked.

"O yes! I want to have a girl and a boy that would love me."

"And I'm sure one day you *will* settle down and have a lovely family of your own." she said. I wiped away a tear.

"It's the onions making me cry." I laughed nervously.

I met a nice boy called Darren De-Barr. His Dad was a well-known local businessman. They lived in a big house. It was very grand. At first I felt awkward and out of place there but they were good to me. I told them my life-story. I had a good story to tell. Everyone felt sorry for me. But it wasn't Love. I think they saw me as the 'poor little orphan'. Mr. De-Barr offered me a job in his office. It was just cleaning and sorting the post although I told my flat mates I was a secretary. I had ambitions. I dreamed of running my own business and going home to a loving husband and children. I would look after them and make them happy.

I didn't hear from my foster family even though I was only living a mile away. I often had to pass their house but I never saw anyone there. I didn't want to look anyway and I didn't want to know.

Then one day as I was walking near their house I heard a voice call me from across the road. A familiar voice that I recognised immediately.

"Lolly-Pop! Hey! Lolly-Pop! What you up to?"

There was only one person who ever called me Lolly-Pop. Nigel was waving and smiling and jumping up and down across the road. He ran towards me, dodging the traffic. His face beaming and his arms held out. He had a new short hair style but he was the same old Nigel. I stood watching. He picked me up, swept me off my feet, swung me round and hugged me fondly.

"I'm *so* pleased to see you!" he cried. "Where have you been? I've been trying to contact you. No-one knew where you were."

I could hardly answer. I remembered how much I had loved him. Feelings of emotion and excitement overwhelmed me but I tried not to show it.

He released his tight hold on me. His arms relaxed.

"Where have you been?" he asked again.

I told him where I was living and asked him what he had been doing since we last met.

"I've been missing *you*." he replied with a grin. "Oh yeah! I did move away for a while. My Mum told you all about it didn't she. It didn't work. We split up. Oh, Lolly-Pop I'm so sorry I hurt you. My poor, dear Lolly-Pop, I live back home now with my Mum again. I was sorry to hear about your family. Mary and Len have split up. Mary still lives in the house with the two children. Well, they are not children anymore. Katy is off to university soon I think. Len goes to visit them sometimes. I went round to ask them for your address. They said they didn't know where you were. Was that really true or were they just trying to protect you"

"No. That was true. I don't want *them* to know where I'm living. I'm on my own now. I don't need them."

"Is there a man in your life? Are you married yet?" He spoke quickly, excitedly.

"Married?! You must be joking! I am only just seventeen. I have no intention of getting married . . . . until I meet the man of my dreams that is." We both laughed.

"I want to see you again. Please." he asked and looked into my eyes. "I could be the man of your dreams."

"I'm not sure." I answered cautiously and dropped my gaze.

"I take you out for a drink tonight. I'll pick you up at eight o'clock on the corner. Please come!" He sounded determined.

"I'll be there." I replied.

*   *   *

We met that evening and it was so good being with him again. We had lots to talk about. I told him about my flat mates and about my job in the office in town.

"Where's your lovely long hair?" I asked him.

"I had to have it cut for work." he replied. "Something to do with health and safety. I'm still working in the same place but I've a bit more responsibility now. I needed to look smarter." I laughed.

"You always look smart." I told him. He reached across and took my hand.

"I've really missed you. I can't believe you are here with me now. I did so want to see you again. I was a fool to let you go."

I was embarrassed and didn't know how to answer.

"I was only fourteen when I met you. I kept that note you sent me for years. The one that said: '*Dear Lolly-Pop!*' Eventually I got rid of it. I burned it. When you moved away it was the end of an era in my life."

"I'm so sorry I hurt you. I didn't know what I was doing. I knew you were still at school. My Mum and your Mum both said you needed to concentrate on your school work. I hope you did well in your exams. You're really clever."

"No." I replied. "I never did the exams. I had to move out. Social Services found me the flat. It's a type of hostel."

We talked and talked until the pub was closing. We walked back to the car.

"What happened to your yellow sports car?" I asked.

"Aah! It had to go. It got too old and worn out, too expensive to run. I gave it to my brother and he ran it for a while. This blue Fiesta is much more reliable. It's not new but it goes well. Come on I'll take you home."

We sat in the car outside my flat still talking. I thought about inviting him in but then thought he would probably get the wrong idea. He put his arm around me and pulled me close. He spoke quietly and lovingly.

"This is where you belong, here in my arms. We could be an item again. You and me. What do you think?"

"I like being with you." I replied cautiously.

"Then I'll see you again tomorrow night. Pick you up at eight."

"No, not tomorrow. I've got to . . . er . . . wash my hair." I knew it was a feeble excuse. It was all I could think of.

"Then I'll pick you up the next night. See you at eight on the corner."

"O.K." I replied. I kissed him gently on the cheek, got out of the car and went indoors. My flat mates were waiting for me. They wanted to know all about him.

I hadn't had a nightmare for ages but that night my dreams were vivid.

NOCTURNE

"Laura-Louise! Laura-Louise!" My Mother's voice is calling me. I can hear her but she is a long way away.

"Mummy!" I reply. "Mummy! Where are you?"

I try to run. My legs pound backwards and forwards but it is like running on a cloud. I don't get anywhere. Mist swirls about my feet.

"Laura-Louise! Laura-Louise!" The voice changes.

"Lolly-Pop! Hey! Lolly-Pop! Come here. Come to me!"

Blue and yellow cars race between us, their engines revving noisily. I try to cross dodging the traffic but it is hopeless. I have to go back. A yellow car screeches to a halt. I run towards it and look inside for the driver. At first the vehicle seems empty.

'There must be a driver.' I see the shadowy figure at the wheel. His face is dark, marred and twisted. He grinned maliciously, shook his long hair and turned away. The engine revs angrily and the car speeds away.

"Lolly-Pop! Hey! Lolly-Pop! Come over here!" The voice calls me again. The traffic is too much. Too many cars. Too close. Too noisy.

"Look out!" I shout. "It's a dangerous road."

Someone is trying to cross towards me. "Stop! Look out!" I call again but I watch my words drift away on the mist.

There is a screech of brakes. I wait for the crash. When it comes I know someone is hurt. I can't scream. I can't speak. I stand there. Somebody should call for an ambulance. Everything is dark.

Yellow cars racing by become golden balls, more and more, millions of them sweeping past me, overwhelming me until I cannot stand. I lay down as they power over me.

Then everything is dark again.

I awoke to the sound of an ambulance passing my window.

CHAPTER 19

'R ape' is a terrible word.
I had told Nigel that I was 'washing my hair.'
It wasn't strictly true. I couldn't meet him because I was
seeing someone else. Clive was sweet. I quite liked him but
he wasn't Nigel. As I got ready to meet him I made up my
mind that I would not see him again. I knew that I would
much rather be with Nigel.

We were sitting in Clive's tiny bed-sit sipping cider and
listening to Whitney Houston's music. I began to explain
that I would not be able to see him again. Our relationship
was not going anywhere. I wanted to concentrate on my
work and maybe get some qualifications. I rambled on
trying to explain tactfully that I did not wish to see him
again. Suddenly he grabbed me. His strength overpowered
me. He was angry. He held me tightly and passionately but
not lovingly. I tried to crawl away. He pulled at my clothes
and forced me to the floor.

Rape is a terrible word.

I felt dirty. I left in silence and walked alone back to
my flat. I could see the gentle rain slanting in the beams
of light from the street lamps. I didn't speak to anyone. I
didn't know who to speak to. No-one would believe me.
'Clive was sweet. Everyone liked him.' I put all my clothes
in the washing machine and climbed into bed. I pulled the
duvet up over my head and wondered why I couldn't cry. I
had a shower then lay on the bed again. How could I ever

tell Nigel what had happened? I knew the facts of life. I remembered what Mum had told me about 'the birds and the bees'. She had talked about Love. This was not how I had planned to 'grow up'. I had lost my innocence to a thieving brute. How could men be so insensitive? Were all men as forceful and selfish as Clive? I never wanted to see him ever, ever, *ever* again as long as I lived. I thought again about my foster family. I thought about my brother Andrew. I wondered where he was. And then I began to cry. I sobbed into my pillow.

I woke up crying. There had been many times when I had cried myself to sleep but I had never before woken up crying. I felt sick and the pain within me was indescribable. I stood looking in the mirror. My hair was a mess. I picked up the scissors and began to cut it, slowly at first then frantically hacking away until hanks of long black locks lay on the floor. The morning sun flashed across the mirror. Suddenly, without warning, a spasm of epileptic seizure threw me to the bed. I knew I thrashed arms and legs. When it was over I lay still for a while breathing deeply. My mind and memory slowly returned. The horror of the previous evening swept into my head.

Rape is a terrible word. No, 'Rape' is not just a word. Rape is hell.

I got myself up, washed and dressed carefully, tidied my short hair as best I could and made my way to work. I had stopped seeing Darren De-Barr a while ago but his parents were still very good to me. They kept me on at work in their office just part time but at least it was work and they paid me well. Gradually I was given more responsibility. I enjoyed using the computer and sometimes I was asked to write letters, check accounts or answer the telephone. My confidence grew. I didn't tell anyone about my experience with Clive. Work was my escape from the realities of life.

I didn't even tell Nigel.

I began to see him regularly. It was like coming back home. I just loved being with him. I felt that I knew him so well and he knew me. He was good to me but I did have secrets.

I determined to be happy, to smile and to make the most of my youth. Youth was meant to be enjoyed and was going to enjoy it. My stubborn attitude was sometimes a blessing.

The next couple of weeks passed without great incident. I didn't see Clive again. Ever. I enjoyed the work at the office and I especially enjoyed being with Nigel again. We became closer but I didn't like it when he got too close.

I was so excited to be back with Nigel but my fits were getting worse. Nigel suggested I went back to the doctor to ask his advice. I was not really concentrating on my work. I was neglecting cleaning the flat and when I got in I was too tired to clean the kitchen and put out the rubbish. The bathroom was getting embarrassingly filthy. My flat-mates asked what was wrong.

"Nothing!" I replied. "I'm just so tired. I'm out with Nigel every evening and I'm very happy. I'm fine."

"Your fits are getting worse." they observed. "We all think you should see the doctor."

"Well it's nothing to do with any of you. I'm just tired. That's all."

But I did go to see the doctor. I told him about my fits and how tired I was. He asked all the usual questions. I answered as honestly as I could. He examined me carefully.

I left the surgery to walk home thoughtfully. I needed to make some decisions.

On the way back I had to walk past our old house, my foster home. I knew that Mary still lived there. I would never call her 'Mum' any more. I didn't even think of her as 'Mum.' She had hurt me and rejected me. She was not my Mum. I looked across at the house. Same old curtains at the window. Same old roses growing in the garden. It all looked so familiar. I looked up at my old bedroom window. I wondered what it was like inside. What did Mary do now? And what about Katy and little David? Gosh! **Little** David would not really be 'little' any more. If I'm seventeen, he must be fifteen! Time was racing by. I thought about them all. It must have been a big decision for them to take in two more children. Andrew and I could not have been easy.

I found myself walking across the road, opening the front gate, walking up the path and knocking on the familiar front-door. I waited. Gosh! Whatever was I doing here? Maybe they were all out. They wouldn't be pleased to see me after all this time. It was more than a year. I must turn and leave quickly.

But then the door opened and Mary was there. I watched the expression on her face when she saw me. She smiled! She really smiled! It was a big, happy beaming smile. She called out:

"Laura-Louise! Laura-Louise! My Goodness! How wonderful to see you! Come in! Come on in!"

I stepped inside. The house had not changed at all. Mary had not changed. Not really. She did seem genuinely pleased to see me.

"Come out to the kitchen. Would you like a cup of tea?

You must come and tell me all about yourself and what you have been doing since I last saw you. I have been worried about you. I didn't know where you were and Social Services wouldn't tell me."

I followed her through the house and sat at the old scrub-top table while she made the tea. She made it just the way I like it and she hadn't needed to ask. She put some custard creams on a plate and I helped myself.

"Are you all right?" I asked nervously. I didn't really know what to say. I didn't really know why I was here. I needed someone to talk to.

"We are all fine. Thank you. I am much better now. It's just me and Katy and David here now. But tell me about yourself. I like your new, shorter hair style. Where have you been?

Somehow I misinterpreted this last question.

"I've just been to the doctor. I still go to the surgery just along the road here. I was walking past the house and thought I'd call in to see you. I've got some news."

"What's that?" she inquired curiously.

"I've just been to the doctor and . . . I'm pregnant."

CHAPTER 20

"I don't want this baby!" I tried to stifle the tear than ran down my cheek. "I really don't want to have a baby. I only went to the doctor because my fits were getting worse. I don't want to have a baby."

"What does Nigel say?"

"*Nigel*?! O no! It's not Nigel's. He doesn't know. He mustn't know."

And then I began to tell her the whole, long story and Mary just sat there across the table listening. When I had finished, I looked at her closely and wondered if she really believed me. Eventually she spoke.

"Can you be sure it's not Nigel's baby? I heard that you were back together."

"Absolutely! Definitely. It cannot possibly be Nigel's."

"Have you been to the police? You would have good reason."

"I don't want to." I said bluntly.

"What do you want to do?"

"I just want it to go away. I want to get rid of it. The doctor said I have good reason to have an abortion." My voice was fading. "I am only seventeen . . . . I was raped . . . . I am on my own and I have epilepsy. I want an abortion."

Mary stood up and hugged me. Just at that moment in time, I needed a Mum and Mary is the nearest I have to a Mum.

"Are you sure that's what you want?"

"I'm quite sure. But the doctor says it would cost a lot of money. I would probably have to pay for it myself. I don't know what to do."

"I've always been opposed to the whole idea of abortion. You know my views. Maybe I need to rethink my own policies. I know I could never have had an abortion myself. Having children has been the best thing I have ever done in my life. Most parents would tell you the same. Your own Mother loved you so much Dear. She would never have wanted you to have endured all you have been through without her being there beside you. I can never be her. I am not your real Mum but I am the nearest you've got. We invited you into our family. You are still my daughter. I think of you as a daughter. You are a part of this family. If you are sure that an abortion is what you really want, and if we have to pay for it then we will do that." I looked at her closely. Was she really offering to pay for it? I knew her views on the subject. She would never have been happy about abortion.

"Do you really mean that?" I asked.

"If that is what you really want. Next time you go to the doctor talk to him about it. How many weeks are you?"

"Six weeks.""Then we must get things moving quickly. You talk to the doctor again tomorrow and give him my telephone number. I will speak to him and I will see that everything is arranged. It's a very simple operation these days. Just a short spell in a clinic or a hospital."

Just then I heard a key in the front door and someone came in. Mary called out.

"Katy! Katy! Come into the kitchen! Guess who's here!"

She stood up and put an arm gently round my shoulder. She whispered in my ear:

"Don't you worry about anything. It's all going to be fine."

When I saw Katy I was surprised at just how much she seemed to have changed. She was taller and more confident. She was wearing more makeup than I remembered her using before. Her hair was still long and blond and her figure more willowy than ever. When she saw me she bounced up and down with delight.

"Wowee! *Lol?"* She exclaimed! "*Lolly*!" This was her pet name for me; a corruption of the name that Nigel had given me. "That's brill, brill, *brill . . . . !"*

Her voice got louder and higher with excitement. She threw her arms around me. "Boy! I've so missed you? Are you coming back home? I miss our long chats."

This was not at all the reception I had expected. I didn't know how to react. It was all so different from the day we had all parted. The bitterness of that day was still painful. I remembered that it was Mary that had arranged for us to move out and live somewhere else. I hadn't even noticed that she had been getting more and more depressed. I hadn't noticed that their marriage was suffering. Everyone always said, 'What a lovely family!' I guess no-one noticed the reality. The stress of having four stroppy teenagers in the house must have taken its toll.

Katy went to 'fridge and poured herself a glass of fruit juice.

"D'you want one of these?" she said as she held up the glass to me.

"No, thank you. I've just had a cup of tea and some biscuits. I've been talking to . . . er . . . Mary.

"Have you got time to come upstairs and see my bedroom? It's just been decorated. It looks really great. Come up and we can have a chat. I want to know what you've been doing."

So I went upstairs. I wasn't in a hurry. I was comfortable with Katy. I felt at home. I sat on her bed listening to her music.

"Hey!" she said, "Do you remember this music? We used to play it so much till Mum got fed up with it and told us off." She put on the music of our old favourites. "And guess what? I had a letter from Mark,—remember Nigel's friend. He wants to see me again! I thought 'no-way!' I didn't even reply. You used to call him 'Dimbo' because he was so thick!" We both laughed. "I'm seeing a boy called Matthew now."

"I've still got my doll." I said. "do you remember the game we always played with them?"

Katy went to the cupboard, rummaged around a bit and then pulled out her old doll, looking rather more tatty than I remembered. We both laughed again. I was good being with her. We sat there for ages talking about the times we had had together. She asked me about Andrew. I had to admit that I missed him terribly. I didn't know where he was.

"Mum misses him too. She went all the way to Brighton looking for him because someone told her that he'd been seen there working in a supermarket. She went in the shop but didn't see him. I think she went back again a week later but she never found him. I don't know what she would have done if she'd seen him. She's been trying to find you too. The social worker wouldn't say where either of you were."

"I've been living on the other side of the town, not far from here. Sometimes I've had to walk past the house. It was really strange. The house is just the same as it always was."

"Yeah! It doesn't change much except my room's been decorated. The house seems very big and empty now there's only us three here and soon I shall be leaving and going to uni. The house will be very strange then."

"What's my old room like? I'd like to se it?""Come on then! It's no different really—Oh, except it's **tidy**!"

"What a cheek! I was the tidy one! Mum used to say that if ever anything went missing she's always look for it under **your** bed!" We both giggled. I hadn't noticed that I had slipped back to calling her 'Mum'.

My old bedroom was almost the same.

"Someone's moved the bed!" I exclaimed. "It used to be over there."

"Oh, yes. I think Mum moved it when she vacuumed the room. Look! The bed's still made up so that when visitors come they can stay in here."

"What? You mean that other people have been staying in **my** room?"

"Just Aunty Sylvia and Dorothy. They came to stay for a few days last Summer. I think there are still some of your old toys in the wardrobe. You left them behind and Mum won't get rid of them."

We explored the memories in the wardrobe. The musty smell of those old toys really took me back to my childhood.

"If ever I have children . . . ." I began . . . and then I remembered. How could I possibly have forgotten?

"What's wrong?" asked Katy when she saw my sudden confusion.

"I came here to tell people my news. You see, . . . I was raped . . . and now I'm pregnant . . . and I don't know what to do."

CHAPTER 21

I t was very late when I got back to my little flat that night. I had stayed at Mary's for dinner and Katy and I had talked and talked. The girls at the flat never asked how I got on at the doctor's; perhaps they had suspected the news or more likely they didn't really care.

Now I had renewed my relationship with Mary I visited them often. I met Len and David again too. At fifteen, David was now taller than any of us. It was a reserved and icy reception at first. I was surprised, but gradually old hurts were healed. Mary came with me to talk to the doctor. I explained that I wanted an abortion. It all happened so quickly I didn't really have time to worry about it.

Mary came to visit me at the hospital. I awoke to see her sitting there beside me. I was very drowsy. I couldn't see properly. There was a dull ache inside.

"How do you feel?" she asked.

"I don't think I've had it done yet." I murmured.

"Yes, you have." she replied. "It's all over now Love."

I shut my eyes and slept.

Of course, I had to tell Nigel my news. I didn't know how he would react but the truth was a shock. I told him exactly what had happened. I even told him the details that I had not told anyone else.

. . . And he didn't believe me! He thought I had been unfaithful to him. I hadn't. He didn't want to see me after that.

I was fed up with the other girls at the flat. The social worker came to visit us often. She explained that once I was adult she would not need to visit me. More than that, I would have to find somewhere else to live.

"This flat is a hostel for girls who are supported by Social Services." she explained. Once you are eighteen you are considered an adult. I will not need to visit you. You will be able manage on your own, I know you can."

She reminded me that I did have a job. I would be entitled to some benefits so I should be able to afford rent on a council flat but when she showed me the prices and places that were available to me I knew it was out of the question. Every flat I considered was either too far away for me to get to work or much too expensive. With my epilepsy I would never be able to drive a car.

"Who would pay rent like that?" I asked but she had no reply.

It seemed I was on my own for real this time. 'So where do I go now?' I asked myself. 'What else can go wrong in my Life? Who can I turn to?'

Surprisingly, it was Katy who came to my rescue. She was planning her eighteenth birthday party when I explained my dilemma.

"Then you must come back home and live with us!" she said very definitely.

"But I can't ask Mary to have me back. She was the one who arranged for me to leave in the first place."

"She was ill. It was depression. She couldn't cope. She's much better now. She's given up the teaching job. It got too stressful. What with us as stroppy teenagers too. Money is a bit tight. Everyone thinks they get lots of money for fostering but Mum said they don't get anything. Nothing! Zilch! Not a penny! It's because it's private fostering or something. So, Social Services have looked after you at the hostel, and now you are an adult. It's all different now we are growing up. You must come back here to live. Please! Say you will?"

I was dumbfounded.

"I don't dare ask her if I could come back here to live."

"Would you like to?" I nodded and smiled.

"Then *I'll* ask her! Best time to ask is when she's busy . . . then she won't have time to think. She'll say 'Yes' anyway. I know she will. Come on, come on, she's busy in the kitchen now. It's now or never!"

Katy did all the talking. She knew just how to approach her Mum. It was all arranged without me having to say anything. I didn't know what to say anyway. I just politely said 'Thank you.' Then I tentatively asked:

"Will I be able to have my old room?"

"Of course you can. It's all there just the same waiting for you. There are even some of your toys in the cupboard. There's the same wallpaper up. I expect you'll think it a bit childish now. We could decorate it again if you like."

I said 'Thank you again.' and went back to flat to sort out my things there. I didn't have much. There were a few precious ornaments that had belonged to my Mother, a few clothes and my makeup and washing things, that's all.

I said a quiet 'goodbye' to the other girls at the flat.

"You're not moving out, are you? You can't leave us! Who will clean up after us? Who will wash up and put the clean mugs back in the cupboard? And who will clean the loo?"

"You'll have to do it yourselves." I said and I had no

sympathy for them. They clearly had no sympathy for me either.

So I moved back into my old room at Mary's house. I shifted the bed back to it's old position under the window and on the wall I stuck the old photograph of my Mother. Beside my bed I placed my medication, my clock and my picture of Mother with Andrew and me when we were very small. I hung my clothes neatly in the wardrobe. I put my make-up on the dressing table and adjusted the mirror so that I could not see my reflection when I sat up in bed. That dazzling reflection always made me feel I was going to have another fit. The old wallpaper was of woodland animals. Yes, I suppose it was a bit childish but I didn't want to change it. Not yet anyway. I wanted the room just the way it had been. When everything was in place I looked out of the window but there was no yellow car. Some things have to change. I thought about Nigel. I knew he had a blue car now but there was no sign of him. At least from this window I could watch out for him. He would be coming home to his Mum's house every evening. I looked at the clock. Another hour and he would be home. I must remember to look out of the window then. He wouldn't want to see me. He still thought I had been unfaithful to him. I would watch him.

It was surprisingly easy settling back into life in the big, old Edwardian house. It was where I had spent my childhood, where I had grown up. I made myself at home. I knew where everything was kept in the kitchen and I could help myself to tea and biscuits. Katy seemed to prefer fruit juice these days. She said she tried to keep a healthy diet but I noticed there were packets of crisps and sweets in her room. David still had his attic room and he always seemed to have crowds of noisy friends up there. They were all drinking and smoking although he was still under age. He played his loud heavy-metal music and the bass beat throbbed through the house. I would hear his big feet stomping round the house in tatty boots and thundering down the stairs past my room. He didn't say much to me. He wasn't the cute little brother that I remembered. I don't think he deliberately avoided me, he just had other things on his mind.

Katy and I still got on like the proverbial 'house on fire.' We had so much to talk about. Mary was polite, sometimes too polite. She cooked meals for us although we rarely all sat down to eat together. Sometimes I helped her wash up and this was a chance to talk. She chatted to me but often her conversation was about Katy, *her* examination results, *her* applications to university and *her* plans to be a teacher. I began to resent the bragging.

One evening I stood at the window in my room watching the cars pass. It was nearly twenty past five. Mary breezed into the room.

"*Oh Laura!*" she exclaimed angrily when she saw me, "Sometimes I think you only moved back in here so that you could spy on Nigel from the window!" She stormed out again with a huff of resentment. I was furious. The accusation was too close to the mark. I moved from the window and lay on my bed listening.

Katy came rushing in to my room excitedly.

"Hey! Guess what?" She didn't notice my feelings. "Guess what?" she cried again. "I've had a letter from Mark! D'you remember Mark, Nigel's friend? He says he wants to see me again . . . . after all this time. And you wouldn't believe what he writes about how he's missed me and the graphic details of what he'd like us to do!" She showed me the letter and we both giggled again.

"He's got a nerve, expecting me to go back to him. I shan't take any notice of the letter of course. I'm not even going to bother to reply. Anyway I'm seeing Simeon tonight. We're going to a club." She flicked her long, golden hair out of her eyes.

"*Simeon*?!" I was surprised. "I thought you were going out with someone called Matthew!"

"Oh yes, I am. But I'm seeing Sim tonight. He is gorgeous! So good looking! *And* he's going to uni. Sadly, probably not the same one as me. We get on really well. Why don't you come out with us?"

"No. Thank you but I couldn't. I'd feel like a gooseberry!"

"O.K. See you later! I need to get ready." Katy took her letter from Mark, waved it at me, giggled and skipped out of the door. I heard her in her own room playing her music and singing along with it. She was happy. Everything was going well for her. I wondered about my future. I had no qualifications now, no prospects and now no Nigel either. I missed him.

CHAPTER 22

I missed my brother Andrew too. He was so special to me. I needed him. I wondered where he was and what he was doing. It was thoughtless of him to leave me,—to just run away like that. It was selfish. Someone had told Mary that he had gone to live in Ireland with his real Dad. I didn't know. I hadn't heard from our real Dad for years now. Had Andrew been in touch with him? Maybe he had been in touch secretly all the time. Did Andrew have a secret too that he couldn't even tell me? Dad had always said that I was the special one. He called me 'Sweetheart' and we had a secret. Would I still be special to him? Would he still call me 'Sweetheart'?

I was beginning to feel that my life was one list of disasters. I must have been very bad. What had I done to deserve all this? It was bad enough when Mother and Father split up and I didn't even remember that. I was only five. I knew it had been hard. Mother was sad. Yet she was happy at the same time. She was glad that he had gone.

Then when my Dear Mother died I cried and cried but I didn't understand. I tried to be good when I moved in with Mary and Len and their children. I really did try to be good. I even called them Mum and Dad from the very moment I became a part of their family, so when they split up too I wondered, was it all my fault? Did I have this effect on people? Did I turn their worlds upside down so that they could not cope, not even with each other? It must be me.

I stood up and looked in the mirror. I wasn't the sweet little girl that my Dad would remember. I had put on weight. I had teenage spots. My long, dark hair was tangled over my shoulder. It needed cutting. I grabbed a fistful of hair and piled it up on top of my head, then I dragged it all back behind my ears and held it in place with my hands. What would it look like short, very short? I made a decision to have it completely restyled. I would find a really good hairdresser. It might be expensive but I needed a new image. I couldn't admit that what a really wanted was a new me.

I went to the bathroom and washed my face with lots of soap. I rubbed it in until my face was red and sore. I looked in the mirror again. The light glanced off the bright surfaces. Hastily I turned off the taps. I needed Nigel. I needed someone who knew me well. Then everything faded into oblivion. The seizure took hold of me and threw me to the floor. When I regained consciousness my head ached and Katy was banging on the bathroom door.

"Laura! Come on! Hurry up! I need the bathroom! I'm going out."

I opened the door. Katy was standing there.

"Katy!" I said, "You look lovely! Have fun with Simeon!" and I went back to my room. I lay on the bed listening and thinking. Outside I heard a car engine start up and pull out. I rushed to the window and from behind the curtain I could see Nigel driving. And there was someone else in the car with him. I was racked with jealousy. *I* had been in that car. *I* had sat in that seat with Nigel beside me at the wheel. Who was he with? Where were they going? Did he know I was watching? Was he doing this to deliberately torment me?

The next day, sitting in the hairdresser's chair I had time

to think. I don't like the loneliness of not knowing who I am. I need a new image. Mr De-Barr was very good to me even though I wasn't going out with his son any more. He gave me extra hours work in their office. I'm beginning to understand more of the finance business. I can answer the telephone and sometimes give advice. The other staff are pleased with me. I'm becoming a workaholic. Life is a bit of a whirl but it's all an illusion. Much of my stubborn determination to impress is borne out of not knowing who I am. I've become used to being part of a big family but I like being on my own.

"Are you sure you really want it cut short?" The hairdresser interrupted my thoughts.

"Oh, er . . . . yes please. Cut it really short and shaped into the neck at the back. Perhaps it could be shaped around my ears too."

"You have such lovely, shiny dark hair. You're lucky. Lots of girls would love to have hair as thick and healthy as this." She picked up the scissors. I didn't want to talk. I returned to my thoughts about Andrew. I would like to try to find him. I will ask his old friends and maybe an old Aunt would know where he was. It had been a big decision to move back into the house with Mary. That old house held so many memories. I tried to think of the happy times of my childhood. It was hard to remember things. I could remember the holidays in Cornwall with Grandma. I remembered silly things,— like the time she bought me a flowery swimming hat and I refused to wear it. Like the time Andrew fell in a rock pool with all his clothes on. I remembered our primary school days and my friends there and the dinner lady who was always nice to me and gave me sweets.

I looked up and glanced in the mirror before me. The hairdresser was talking. I hadn't been listening. Her scissors snipped and dark locks cascaded to the floor. The bright light flashed in the mirror and bounced back to my eyes. I felt my head spinning.

"I don't feel very well." I said. "I think I'm going to . . ."

When I regained my senses I was sitting on the floor with lumps of my own hair stuck to my clothes. Someone was gazing down at me. I couldn't think who it was. It took me a few minutes to think.

"I'm sorry." I said.

"Are you OK now? Would you like a drink of water? She helped me up and I sat in a chair.

"D'you want me to carry on cutting your hair?"

"Yes please. I'm better now. I can't go home half-cut can I?"

She giggled. Everyone laughed, even the other clients sniggered quietly but I wasn't sure what was funny.

She continued to cut my hair in silence. I tried to remember what I had been thinking about before the seizure. When I looked back in the mirror I hardly recognised myself. My hair was completely restyled, short and spiky on top and I could see my ears. I thanked her politely although I was not sure that I liked it now. It was expensive. I was glad of the extra money I earned at the De-Barr's office. On the way home I bought a pair of long, dangly earrings and wore them straight away. I waited for the reaction at home.

Mary looked very surprised then said she liked it because it made me look more grown up and sensible. Katy just said "Wow!" and David didn't even seem to notice. I had hoped for more of a response than that. Katy was more interested in talking about her evening out with Simeon.

"He's so gorgeous!" she enthused. "We had a wonderful time. We get on so well together. He wants to see me more often! And I want to be with him too. He could be really special. He could be *the* one . . . I just wish . . . . I just wish there was somewhere . . ." She took a deep breath, almost a sigh. "I wish there was somewhere we could go . . . where we could be alone. I *can't* invite him back here to my bedroom can I? There's always someone else here. He says he can't invite me back to his bedroom either. His parents are very strict. They wouldn't approve. It's hopeless. Hopeless. I don't know what to do but I know he is the most special boyfriend for me. I really want him to be *more* special. You know what I mean? My first . . . er . . . *experience*!" She sighed again.

"There is *somewhere* you could go." I whispered. She didn't seem to listen. She had turned to look in my mirror. She picked up my hair brush and was pulling her hair back to see what it would look like really short.

"There *is* somewhere you could go." I repeated.

"What? Where?" She turned and replaced the hairbrush.

"I've still got my old flat at the hostel with the other girls. It's empty. It's only mine for two more days. You could go there."

She thought for a moment then smiled shyly. She pulled her long fair hair back over her face and shoulders and shook it into place.

"Yeah?" she queried. "Really? Do you think we could go there?"

"It'd be really private. No-one would disturb you."

"What would I tell people? What would I tell my Mum?"

"You don't tell her anything."

"She likes to know where I am."

"Then tell you are going up to my old flat to collect some of my things I left there."

Katy smiled and held her breath for a few seconds.

"When?" she asked.

"Tonight?" I replied.

She was silent for a few thoughtful moments then she smiled again and hugged me.

"You're an angel!" she declared.

"No I'm not!" I grinned. "I'm wicked old witch!"

CHAPTER 23

One day, soon after that, something amazing happened. The home-coming was just the best thing that had happened to me for a very, very long time. He just turned up! One afternoon, there he was on the doorstep. Mary had been washing up and she answered the door, tea-towel in hand to see Andrew standing there grinning. It was as though he'd never been away.

"Andrew's home!" I shrieked when I saw him. "Andrew's home!" I wanted to give him a big hug but I hesitated. I felt I didn't know him any more. I wasn't sure. Then he came and wrapped his strong arms around me and for the first time I can remember he kissed me. My dear, big brother kissed me. He stayed all that evening and then went back to his flat about an hour's bus ride away. The next weekend he came again and asked if he could stay the night. He slept in his old bed, in his old room. And the next weekend he stayed two nights. And the next weekend he just stayed. He never went back.

It was sometime before I got the whole story out of him. He **had** been working in a supermarket and yes . . . he **had** been seeing our Dad and yes . . . . he **had** been to Ireland . . . but only for a holiday.

"The Prodigal Son has returned!" declared Mary. "We ought to kill the fatted calf and celebrate! Let's have a big party!"

They say that human beings are the only creatures on earth that let their children come back home. I wondered why there was no big party when I came back to this house. Why such a celebration for Andrew? What about me? Do I get a party?

We did have a big party. Actually it was Katy's eighteenth birthday party. There were loads of people. I invited the girls from my flat at the hostel but none of them came. Andrew's old friends were there. Katy's friends were there and I knew lots of them from school. They were pleased to see me. Andrew was surprised that so many girls from our school days had grown into beautiful young ladies! I think he rather fancied one of them. He was with her all through the party. Len was there too and he danced with Mary. they did a funny old jive. He made a speech and said how wonderful it was to have all the family together again. He was good at making speeches. He proposed a birthday toast to Katy. Soon she would be leaving to go to university.

"This party," he announced "Is for the whole family. We welcome back to the fold out lovely Laura-Louise," he raised his glass in my direction, "And the handsome young Andrew." Then there was another toast; "To The Family . . . ."

We raised our glasses of champagne and echoed: "To The Family!"

I was pleased to be there. I was part of a family once again. I swigged the sparkling champagne and felt it go to my head.

Someone shouted: "Laura's having a fit again!" I was lifted into an arm chair and told not to have any more drink. Just as things start to look good and settled I am reminded that nothing is certain in this life. I am not in control. I spent the rest of the party curled up in the chair with a glass of orange juice. Katy looked stunning in a virginal white lace dress and silver shoes. Simeon was wrapped around her and I watched them smooching through the crowds to the sound of her favourite band. I went to bed about midnight and lay there listening to the throbbing beat of the music until gone 2.00 a.m.

Sometimes I stand at my window and just stare. I see busy people, going about their daily routine, families, children, workmen, businessmen, fussing mothers with toddlers . . . and I wonder if they have as much trauma and pain in their lives as I have experienced. I watch the clouds drifting past the chimney pots. At night I stand and watch as the street-lights flickering into life and in the neighbours' houses I see lights in cosy rooms. Silhouetted figures close the curtains to continue their mysterious lives in secret. Somewhere out there, is there an angel for me?

Sometimes I stand and silently scream inside my head. I cry out to my dear mother.

"Mummy! Mummy! *Why* Mummy?"

She would know the answer. She would sing: 'Didn't we have a lovely time the day we went to Bangor.' She would sing while she danced with the vacuum cleaner; sing and dance and laugh. I have nothing to sing about. When I have children of my own I shall make sure they have happy lives.

That night after the party, I slept erratically. In the early hours of the morning I lay there listening to Andrew's noisy snoring in his room across the landing. He had drunk too much. I got up and crept to his doorway. He was sprawled across his bed, relaxed in his boxer shorts, his red hair tousled on the pillow. His smooth freckled skin was glowing. I envied his clear complexion. I walked across the room and stealthily lay down close and warm beside him. He grunted and stirred and flung an arm across me. I got up and returned to my own room. I looked at the photograph of our mother smiling and happy with me and Andrew beside the hydrangea bush in our old garden.

"***Why*** Mummy? Do you know the answers?"

I lay on my side in my bed staring at the picture and then at my packet of pills on the bedside table. The medication was supposed to control my epilepsy. It obviously wasn't working. My fits were as bad as ever. I wondered what would happen if I stopped taking them. Or should I take ***more*** pills? I had three months' supply. At two a day that was nearly two hundred pills. What if I took all of them? Would it solve my problems? I got up again and tip-toed to the kitchen. Amidst the cluttered remains of the party I found a pint-sized glass and filled it with orange juice from the 'fridge. I carried it carefully back upstairs. I placed it beside the packet of pills and sat looking at them.

I thought about the abortion and the baby that might have been, . . . the baby that had been mine for just short time, growing inside me, . . . a part of me. Had I made the right decision? It might have been a little girl. ***My*** little girl! She would have loved me. She would have called me 'Mummy'. I would have named after my own sweet mother. Maybe she would have grown to look just like her. Or maybe, more likely, the child would have grown to look just like its father and I couldn't have borne that. Did I regret my decision? I had not only lost my baby, I had lost Nigel too. And it was all my fault.

I looked again at the pills and the drink. Two hundred pills would solve something.

NOCTURNE

"Mummy! Mummy! *Mummy!*" The children's voices call from all directions. From left and right they call; behind me and before me; above me and below me. Their voices call, plead, plaintively wailing:

"Mummy! *Mummy!*"

Golden balls of light float past moving to the sound of the children's voices. Far away someone is singing:

'Didn't we have a lovely time . . . . Didn't we have a lovely time . . .'

The song drones on tunelessly and still the children call:

"Mummy! Mummy! Where are you?"

I can hear a baby crying. I rise and follow the golden lights drifting through the doorway. Rays of light filter through the trees in a beautiful garden. The sky is clear blue and big pink flowers are wet with morning dew. I can still hear the baby crying. The children are calling and I have to reach them. I feel myself floating, flying, falling.

"Mummy!" they call. "Don't go away!"

It is raining. There are tiny hail stones falling all around me battering my head and arms. I watch the hail stones bouncing on the garden path. Then, they are no longer hail stones but small white pills cascading all around me. I try to catch them in my two open hands. I have a fist full. I push them all into my open mouth but they just melt away. There is nothing left but the sound of the children's voices.

"Mummy! Mummy! Don't go away!"

CHAPTER 24

When I awoke I could hear people busy in the kitchen. There were some voices I didn't recognise. I thought I heard Len's laugh. He had been at the party but now he was living in a flat on the other side of town. Had he stayed overnight? I listened again and realised it was actually David's voice. He sounded just like his Dad. Some of his friends must have slept over. I got up and went onto the landing but met a strange young man coming from the bathroom.

"'Morning." he mumbled as he zipped up his jeans.

I pulled my dressing gown comfortingly around me and watched him go down stairs. I washed, pulled on a long black skirt and a black T. shirt. I put on some make-up. My short dark, spiky hair looked worse than ever. My eyes were red and puffy. I put on more eye-liner and mascara. I didn't look any better but I felt brave enough to go downstairs and see who was there.

"Gosh!" shouted David when he saw me, "The Walking Dead? You look dreadful."

"You look like I feel." said someone I didn't know.

"You gone all Gothic?" quipped the young man I'd seen on the landing.

I just grunted. David was cooking eggs and bacon for a small group of friends who must have stayed the night.

"D'you want the full English breakfast?" he asked me.

"No thanks." I replied. "I'll just have a glass of orange juice."

"Ah! Sorry. It's all gone. Someone must have helped themselves to the whole lot during the night."

"Oh, er . . . yeah. O.K. then. I think I'll go upstairs again."

I returned to my own room. The pint glass of orange juice was still there, untouched beside my bed. I drank some of it and took one of my pills.

I looked out of the window and stood for a while watching the world go by. An old man sat on the low wall opposite. I'd seen him there before. I didn't know anything about him. I assumed he was homeless. I wondered what had gone on in his life that he seemed so destitute. What would I be like when I was old? I didn't want to grow old. My mother never did.

I wandered into Andrew's room. He was in bed quietly staring at the ceiling.

"Hiya!" he called. "Hiya Tubby! So where's my cuppa? I don't think much of the room service in this place." He joked but I didn't laugh. I sat on the edge of his bed. I wanted someone to talk to.

"What do you think will become of us?" I asked. "You and me? Where will we go in life? What will we do?"

"Dunno!" he replied with a shrug. He clearly wasn't feeling philosophical.

I went on:

"Don't you ever wonder what you'll do in life? Do you think you'll ever get married and have children, have a family of your own?"

"Dunno!" he said again.

"But you must think about it sometimes. I want to have children one day. Don't you want to get married?"

"Not really. I think I'll runaway and elope with that girl who was at the party. What was her name?"

"Oh Andrew! You spent the whole evening with her and you can't remember her name! You are terrible! Typical bloke!" I ruffled his red hair and made it really scruffy.

"Here!" he said pushing me away. "Leave my lovely hair alone, just 'cos yours is short and spiky now." He laughed and ruffled my hair in reply.

"We've got to stick together you and me. You are not to run away like that again. Or if you do you must take me with you. I missed you so much when you were away. How could you do that?"

"Mmm. I think I just needed to find out who I was. I spent some time with my Dad. He's on his own now. He's left his family and children. He was good to me. He found me somewhere to live. He helped me get a job and I could go to the pub with him. I tried to talk to him but I don't think he understood."

"You can always talk to me. Do you think our Mum would be pleased with us? What would she have wanted us to do?"

"She wanted us to be happy and to work hard. She said so in that letter."

"Be happy and work hard . . . ." I repeated thoughtfully. "Yes. You're right. I will work hard. I'm going ask Mr. De-Barr for more hours. Perhaps he could teach me about the finance business. It can't be too difficult. What about you?"

"I've got a transfer to the supermarket near here. I'm

going to work there. They said I could train to be a manager if I wanted."

"Andrew! That's brilliant! That means we shall both be working."

"And now, what about that cuppa? Come on Tubby! What about room service? I *need* a cuppa tea."

"I'll get it, . . . just for you!" And I ran downstairs to the kitchen.

*   *   *

The next party was just a few weeks later. It was just for me. I celebrated my eighteenth birthday with my foster family. I asked Andrew for our Dad's address and I sent him a special letter and invitation. He never replied but . . . joy of joys . . . . I was able to contact Robbie and Jenny, our half-siblings. I hadn't seen them since that first visit so long ago. They came to my party and Jenny brought her boyfriend. It was such a delight to meet them again. They were also the natural children of our mother and they remembered her so well. I realised that my memory of my mother was fading. After all, I was only six when she died. I told Jenny that I remembered our mother's pink dressing gown with the big buttons. I remembered her taking her pills and brushing her blond hair. I remembered her singing and dancing with the vacuum cleaner. Jenny said she could recall those things too but she remembered so much more and I needed to hear all about her. We had so much to talk about. She seemed to understand me. She knew just how I was feeling. It was a good party but it was difficult to talk there. We arranged to meet for a day in London where we could spend some real time together.

My confused sadness seemed to lift when I was with Jenny. Everyone said she looked just like me. At last, I had a real sister, not Katy, . . . a **real** sister who looked and felt and grieved like me.

CHAPTER 25

My wedding day dawned bright and hot and sunny,—a glorious Summer's day with blue skies and the scent of freshly mown grass.

I didn't want a church wedding. I had long since given up organised religion. The more I prayed the worse my life became. Now I was twenty-two, working, independent and determined to forget the past and look only to the future. I had no desire for a traditional bridal gown and all that ceremony. I wore a cream coloured suit. I had all I needed in the man at my side. My dream had come true, my lover, my childhood sweetheart, the boy next door.

Nigel looked so smart and proud. I'd never seen him in a suit and tie before. His Mum smiled at me.

"Well," she said, "You've got what you wanted."

Mary and Len had both supported me throughout the months of preparations for my 'Big Day' but I knew exactly what I wanted. It was to be *my* day, *my* plans, *my* dream. Mr and Mrs De-Barr were generous, I had worked for them for six years and the business was flourishing. I had taken on much of the responsibility of running the company and training new staff. They provided the wedding cars and flowers and they helped us furnish the small terraced house that we were renting. Andrew looked so pleased for me. Len had offered to give me away but I wasn't his to give. I just wanted Nigel at my side. We invited my real Dad but he didn't come. Jenny and Robbie came though with their spouses and Jenny's two beautiful children. The family resemblance between Jenny and me was more apparent than ever now we were both adults. I wanted to have time to talk to her again, to tell her that one day Nigel and I will have children. As sisters, we have so much in common and so much to share. We renewed our promise to keep in touch.

The registrar was a kindly, grandmotherly lady who put me at ease but Nigel's voice cracked nervously as he made his vows. I smiled at him reassuringly and squeezed his hand. He stifled a little laugh. He was not used to such formal, public occasions.

The reception at a big river-side hotel was a special time with so many old friends and family there, but my thoughts were always of the one who could not be there. My Mother. She loved to dress in what she called 'high heels and posh frocks.' She loved parties and big, social occasions. On my wedding day I missed her more than ever. The bride's mum has the privilege of hiding under a big hat while wiping away her own tears at the sight of her beautiful daughter. Mary could never fulfil that role.

I had experienced many problems through life. If I had been brought up in a normal, happy family with my natural mum and dad, the many crises would have just been part of life, part of growing up. Instead, in a foster family, each crisis became a trauma. I felt I was on my own.

But now I was not on my own. I had a husband and a home. Nigel and I settled into married life. I am a natural home-maker. It was such a joy to shop for curtains and covers and cushions and to arrange our wonderful wedding gifts. Nigel laughed at me as I took such pleasure in putting new gadgets in our new kitchen and standing colourful bottles tidily on the shelf in the bathroom.

"You could paint the kitchen cupboards." I suggested to him. "They'd look brighter if they were white."

"I've never done ***painting***!" he shrugged.

"You could do it!" I encouraged. "It can't be too difficult."

We bought a big tin of white gloss paint and a small brush. Nigel began painting. It looked a bit messy.

"Aw! I can't do this!" he exclaimed after a few minutes. "It seems much too sticky. Look! This paint is all sticky! It's on the floor, on my fingers. I'm no good at it."

He stopped work, put down the brush and went to the bathroom. I heard the taps running and splashing noises from the bath. I picked up the brush, finished the painting and cleared up.

"What's for dinner?" he shouted from the steamed-up bathroom.

"Fish and chips." I answered quickly.

"Get me a sausage and a pickled onion!" he called from the landing.

o0o

And so began our marriage. We had delayed the honeymoon and planned to go away later in the year when we could afford it but somehow it never happened. One evening, quite late, Nigel was relaxing in his favourite comfortable armchair watching the golf tournament on television when there was a knock at the door. I answered and was surprised to see Andrew there. He often visited but I hadn't been expecting him so late. I could tell he had been drinking but there was something else, something wrong. He looked as though he had been crying.

131

"What's wrong?" I asked immediately. "Come in. Sit down. What is it? What's happened? Are you hurt?"

He didn't take off his coat but wrapped it round him although it was a warm evening. He sat down in an armchair.

"I've got something to tell you." He sounded serious.

"What's happened now?" I asked.

"There's no point in me 'beating about the bush', I've just got to come straight out with it and tell you."

"Tell me what?"

He sat on the edge of the chair, bolt upright and breathed in deeply.

"It's about our Dad. . . . Not Len, our real Dad. Be prepared for a shock. He's . . . . he's . . . er . . . . gone."

"What do you mean 'gone'?"

"He's dead, Sis. Gone. Gone for good. We are orphans now."

Now for most people, the news that their father had died would have been devastating, heart breaking but I have to say, that for me, at that moment I just thought . . . 'Well . . . . I never saw him much anyway. He was never a part of life. Why the big drama? Why all the tears?' Andrew's reaction surprised me.

"So, what happened?" I asked. "Do you know?"

"Get me a cup of tea please. I think I need it. I have more to tell you."

Now all this time Nigel was watching the golf. I suggested that he went to make the tea. He grunted a bit but went to the kitchen. I turned off the television.

"Tell me!" I asked. "Please tell me what's happened."

Andrew wiped his eyes, took a deep breath and said quietly but very clearly,

"He was murdered . . . . Stabbed."

CHAPTER 26

"Murdered?!"** I shouted. "Whatever do you mean, *murdered*?"

Andrew took a deep breath again and there was a long pause. Then he went on:

"There's no easy way to tell you this but this is something I have to do. I must be the one to tell you." He paused again and wiped his face with a big handkerchief. He seemed to be choosing his words carefully.

"Come on!" I encouraged impatiently. "Tell me. I want to know. I need to know." Andrew sighed. His freckled face was very red.

"It happened in Cornwall." he explained. "That's where he lives now . . . . Lives? . . . No, . . . that is the wrong word. That is where he . . . er . . . *was* living. He had a bit of a row with Elliott. D'you remember Elliott? He's eighteen now. Elliott got drunk, came home late from the pub, had a row with Dad, then . . . just picked up a big carving knife . . . and . . . stabbed him . . . once, . . . just once . . . in the stomach. Our Dad bled to death in his own home, on the living room floor, on the carpet." He paused again. "Our Dad was murdered by our half-brother." He stopped and there was silence for a while. I tried to take in the news. It couldn't be true. Not *my* Dad. Things like that don't happen to us. That only happens on television.

"Murder . . . ." I mumbled, trying to get my head around the word. "*Murder?*"

Lots of crazy ideas were swirling about inside my head. I opened my mouth but the feelings in my head didn't turn into words. I looked at Andrew. I had never seen his expression so hurt and yet so blank. He was trying to understand the news too. Eventually I asked:

"So . . . how do you know all this? Are you sure? It could all be a mistake? How did you hear about it? Who told you?" I had too many questions and too many doubts.

"Mary told me." he answered.

"*Mary?!* How on God's earth did she know?"

"She knew yesterday."

"Yesterday?" I exploded. *"Yesterday?* Then why the hell didn't she tell **_us_** yesterday." I was furious. "We should have been the ones to know straight away. Why did she know first and I didn't? She shouldn't have kept it to herself."

"She didn't tell us because she wanted to be sure. She couldn't tell us until she knew it really was our Dad and it really was true. Don't you see that?"

"So how did she know? Who told her?"

"Well, you might find this hard to believe but she heard it on the news. She recognised the name."

"Well, it could have been someone else then, someone with the same name as our Dad. It might not be him. There must be lots of other people with the same name."

"No Love. It's definitely him. We telephoned Cornwall police. It is definitely our Dad."

"But why didn't they take him to hospital?"

"They did."

"So he'll be alright then, won't he. He'll get better."

"No Love. He won't get better. He has gone." Andrew never called me 'Love' so I knew this was serious. "I know we never saw much of him. He wasn't a part of your life much at all. I remember him a bit from when we were little but you are that year younger. You wouldn't remember him much at all. He was never much of a 'Dad' to either of us. But I'm glad I had that short time with him when I went away. He was good to me when he found me a job and a flat. We even went on holiday together. We went to the pub in the evenings. He'd buy me a drink. He liked Guinness. I could chat to him there. He was more like a mate than a Dad. You must try to think of him like that too. Remember the happy times, the times we went to stay with him . . . when we fed the horse at the end of the garden . . . and played in the paddling pool . . . and . . . and what was that funny thing the children used to say?"

"Chilly-on-the-willy!" I replied at once and we both laughed, then I stopped laughing. I shouldn't be laughing.

"That was Elliott. He used to say that."

Nigel came in with a tray of tea and some biscuits neatly arranged on a plate. I wondered if he'd been listening.

"What's up then?" he asked as he sat back down in his armchair. I looked at him. He was my lovely, new husband. I loved him passionately. He was all I had wanted, all I had dreamed about. We hadn't been married long. I opened my mouth to tell him the news but no words came,—only a plaintive, high-pitched wail that I hardly recognised. It was coming from somewhere deep inside my heart.

Then the tears flowed.

I thought of the few times I had seen my Dad. I thought of the 'secrets' that we shared. He had said that he loved me. He called me 'Sweetheart.' He liked me to look pretty and have long, ringlets in my dark hair and red ribbons. There was the time that he wanted me to go and live with him and go to a big, posh school that cost a lot of money. I would have worn a grey blazer and a big hat. But none of that materialised. None of that mattered. I continued sobbing.

Nigel didn't know how to react to my tears. It was Andrew who came over to sit beside me. He handed me the big, white hanky and put a comforting arm around me. I saw that he was crying too.

"It's just you and me now Sis. We're gonna stick together you and me."

I thought back to the time that we had shed tears for our Mother; how we had sat together with Grandma in the big bed. Now, here we were together shedding tears for our Father.

"What will happen next?" I asked eventually.

"I don't know. Apparently, Elliott ran off but the police found him. I think they are questioning him. There seems no doubt that he did it. He's admitted it. I can only think of Elliott as that funny, cute little boy, splashing about in the paddling pool and saying things to make people laugh. I don't think he meant to kill him, do you?"

"I just don't know. I don't know anything any more. We've had so much in our lives. Don't you sometimes wonder what we have done to deserve all this? Why us? Why me? What have I done? I'm only twenty two. Do you sometimes wonder how different things would have been if our Mum had not . . . left us. She didn't want to go away. She never wanted to leave us."

I began to sob again. Andrew was so kind. He just sat silently beside me. Nigel slurped his tea.

"D'you two want this tea now you've asked me to make it?"

"Yes, thank you." said Andrew politely. He reached across and handed me a mug of warm tea. We all sat silently drinking and wondering what to say next. Eventually Nigel spoke.

"D'you mind if I put the telly back on and see the end of the golf?"

I looked at Andrew.

"No." I replied. "We don't mind. You watch the end of the golf."

"One day," Nigel said, "One day I'm going to be a professional golfer. That's what I want. I could be as good as those guys on the telly. You'll see me there . . . . one day."

After Andrew had gone. Nigel came and sat beside me and we cuddled up together. I felt comforted by his warmth. The golf tournament ended and we went upstairs together. He held me tight and kissed me passionately but I pushed him away.

"Not now, Dear. Please, not tonight."

"This is supposed to be our honeymoon."

"But I don't feel like a honeymooner . . . . just not tonight. Not after the shock I've just had. Please, Love. Try to understand how I am feeling."

"You know I mean it, don't you? I really mean it.""Mean what?" I snuggled down beside him under the warm duvet.

"That one day I'm going to be a professional golfer."

NOCTURNE

"Laura-Louise! Laura-Louise!" Once again I heard my mother's sweet voice calling me through the mist. She was always so far away, so inaccessible. I stretched out my arms towards her; I stretched but I could never touch her. I wanted to feel her arms close around me. I needed to feel the comforting safety of her embrace,

"Laura-Louise! Laura-Louise!" she called again. Now her voice was close behind me, just by my right shoulder. I spun round and thought I caught a glimpse of her smile before she disappeared again.

I was standing in the kitchen,—*her* kitchen. I knew it well from early childhood. There were the familiar old cups by the sink. I had almost forgotten them. I sensed the warm, homely aroma of freshly baked fruitcake, straight from the oven. The cake was on the side, still steaming. She had left it there just for me. There is nothing in this world quite like Mum's homemade cake. I could cut myself a slice. I took a knife from the rack on the wall. I chose the biggest, sharpest one. I held it in my hand. It's blade was bright and shining. As I turned it over and over the reflected lights flashed around the room like sparks bouncing off the walls and ceiling. I ran my fingers along its sharp edge. I felt its sting. I cried out in pain as blood flowed from my thumb. I dropped the knife. The blood ran red and free. *My* blood! It dripped onto the clean blade and into the steaming cake. There was too much blood and too many knives. Blood soaked into the carpet, a bright red pool on the floor.

"Laura-Louise!" My mother's voice called me again.

Then, through the mist I heard another voice. I strained to listen, to hear this new message. As the new, harsher voice got nearer, so my mother's voice faded away.

"Come." called the rough voice. "Help me!"

The voice was deep and masculine. There were too many knives and too much blood.

"Help me, Sweetheart."

CHAPTER 27

I awoke when Nigel brought me tea in bed.
"You were tossing and turning all night." he said. "I know you didn't get much sleep so I thought you'd like a cup of tea." Sometimes Nigel could be so thoughtful.

"What's the time?" I asked sleepily.

"It's early, only ten past six, but I couldn't sleep either, not with you being so restless beside me. I think you had another bad dream."

We sat up in bed drinking our tea. He had even brought us some biscuits.

"You had such a shock last night. I'm not surprised you couldn't sleep. That was terrible news about your Dad. I can't imagine how you must be feeling."

I sipped my tea slowly. I was beginning to hope that, in the cool, clear light of the morning maybe the news from Andrew had all been a part of the nightmare. Nigel went on,

"Murder . . ." he mumbled. "Murder? We don't get things like that going on in our family. I guess I was lucky. I had my Mum and my Dad and my brother always there for me. What do you think will happen to Elliott?"

"Hmm. Don't know. Prison, I expect. But he never meant to kill anyone. He was a sweet, funny little boy. Yes, he had a bit of a temper, so did my Dad especially after a drink. I'm sure Elliott never meant it to end like that. It was just a moment of teenage temper. Yeah, prison . . . . that'll be his future for the next few years."

"But *our* future is together." Nigel sounded unusually philosophical.

"Yes. You're right." I smiled. "Thank you Love, Our future *is* together. You and me. One day we shall have children of our own and we will bring them up to be kind and thoughtful and to respect the law. They will be . . . little angels! In the meantime . . . . I'm so glad I've got you Nigel. I need you beside me. *You* are *my* Angel."

"I'm no angel!" he joked. And then he kissed me. "One day we shall have beautiful children of our own." he repeated.

The following few days were like a grey mist around my head. I couldn't see where my life was going. My marriage was strained but my dependence upon my brother deepened to a symbiotic relationship. We needed each other. Life is an adventure. We can learn from our mistakes. We can learn to see things the right way round. I should by now have learned to expect the unexpected.

Only a few weeks previously I had been planning my wedding, now I was planning my father's funeral. Mary offered to drive us to Cornwall. I would have liked Nigel to be there with me but he didn't want to come so it was just the three of us, Mary, Andrew and me. I wondered who else would be there. My Dad's wife and their children. And what about Elliott? How would I react if he was there. I hoped he'd stay away.

It was a long drive and we were silent most of the way. No-one knew what to say. This wasn't the time for small talk. We didn't have anywhere to stay so had to find a Bed and Breakfast place with vacancies. We booked into a small boarding house in a back street. We never said why we were there but it must have been obvious that we were not your usual Summer visitors. It was the beginning of the holiday season. Tourists were in joyful spirits, children with buckets and spades, teenagers with surfboards, pensioners, hand in hand like Darby and Joan. There was a buzz of excitement and the shops in the town were decorated with flowery fashions. Even the weather shone warm and bright which all added to accentuate my depression. It all seemed so incongruous.

The funeral was a simple affair. I hardly recognised our Dad's 'children', They had grown so tall and looked smart in neat suits with white shirts and black ties. Elliott was not allowed to attend. I was told that the police would let him have some private time alone at the grave after everyone else had gone. There was a lot of speculation and gossip about the court case. Everyone agreed that Elliot never meant to kill him. It was all some terrible, terrible mistake. There was no doubt that it was Elliott's fault. He was definitely guilty. He had admitted it. Andrew and I stood at the grave side with the rest of the family. We were grieving with people we didn't know over a father we didn't really know. But we still shed tears. We still felt orphaned and alone.

Mary didn't come to the funeral. She left us to grieve alone but was there to pick us up. Afterwards I didn't know what to do. Should we meet other members of the family and get to know them? Should we all go out for a meal somewhere? What would we talk about? Secretly, what I really wanted, was to go to the beach, to sit in the sun, to pretend to be on holiday but I thought no-one would have understood or approved of that. This was my Dad's funeral, I should be crying. I had run out of tears.

We went back to the B and B, then went out for a meal. I'm sure everyone knew who we were. I felt them pointing and muttering. I heard whispers of "That's the family of that man who was stabbed. Poor things. They must be here for the funeral. Terrible thing to happen. Terrible! Even the police said that things like that don't happen here. This is a quiet, holiday resort. They must be his children."

The next day we drove home in silence.

I was so pleased to get back to the normality of my new husband and my new home. Nigel was there to greet me. He seemed excited.

"Come in! Come on in! I've got a surprise! I've got something to show you. I've been saving up and I've bought something special."

I was tired from my journey.

"You could show me a cup of tea first. That'd be the best thing." I really wanted to tell him about the funeral but he obviously had something else on his mind. He brought me a big mug of hot tea and we sat down together.

"I've got something to show you." he said again. "I've been saving up and I've bought something. You'll never guess what . . . . oh yeah! Have a guess! Go on! Have a guess!"

"Is it a . . . . dishwasher?" I was joking. We would never have had room for one.

"No. It's not a dishwasher. Try again! Go on!"

"Is it a . . . . new car?" The old blue car was for ever breaking down and costing us a lot in repairs to keep it on the road.

"No. It's not a new car! One more guess then I'll tell you." He was bouncing with excitement.

"Is it . . . . ooh! I know! Is it that new fridge-freezer we saw in the shop?"

"No! No! ***No!*** It's not *any* of those! You haven't guessed. I shall have to tell you. I have been saving up for ages and I have bought something really special. Really, really special. It cost a lot of money." He paused to add to the drama of the moment. "It's a . . . complete . . . new . . . set . . . of . . . *golf clubs*! There! You didn't guess *that* did you?"

CHAPTER 28

Nigel was often out playing golf. I was pleased he had found an interest but I discovered it was an expensive hobby. While I was trying to make ends meet and economising he was out on the golf course. I was earning a reasonable salary now. I was able to give mortgage advice but we were still renting our house. I had thoughts of starting a business of my own. The De-Barrs were very good to me but I needed to move on. I talked to Nigel and I made plans to hand in my notice and set up my own finance company but I didn't want to let people down. I could see they had problems of their own. Mr. De-Barr sometimes came to my desk and sat down. He could talk to me. They were under a lot of stress. Business was bad and their marriage was suffering. Their two young sons were often in trouble with the police. When he came to talk to me I never had any helpful advice. Who was I? I was young, newly married and his employee. But I listened and he said that it helped. I knew what it was like to feel rejected and let down.

Then one morning he didn't turn up for work on time. He was never late, as 'reliable as clockwork' we used to say. I had just sat at my desk and switched on the computer when my personal 'phone-line rang. Mr De-Barr was clearly upset. There was a problem. His youngest son had been in a motor-cycle accident. It was serious. He had to go to the hospital. He wouldn't be coming in to work.

"What time shall I tell the others you will be coming in?" I asked.

"I don't think I will be . . ." he replied hesitantly. his voice faded away.

"That's fine Mr. De-Barr." I said. "You go along to the hospital and see Darren. Tell him to get well soon."

I couldn't catch what he said next but he must have put the 'phone down suddenly. I decided that this was my opportunity to show that I could run the office on my own. I would show him that I was quite capable. I pretended that it was my own business. I stood tall and I spoke in a voice like Grandma's posh tones when she told us what to do. I organised the other staff and helped the new young assistant sort a problem on the computer. I offered advice over the 'phone and spoke to a visitor. I was really enjoying the responsibility.

When the 'phone rang again I was expecting it to be Mr. De-Barr with more news of his son's accident. It was a reporter from the local paper.

"I am so sorry to hear about the tragic accident and do offer my deepest sympathies to Mr and Mrs De-Barr. How are they? Can you tell me what exactly happened?"

I was very confused. What did he mean by a 'tragic' accident and 'deepest sympathies'? How was it that so often the Press seemed to get the news before the families? I hid my anxiety. I spoke clearly and confidently.

"I'm very sorry sir." I said. "But I am not able to give you any more information about the accident. Thank you for calling. Goodbye."

I put down the 'phone and wondered what to do next.

My voice had sounded calm and controlled but inwardly I was shaking with fear. Whatever had happened?

At that moment Mr. De-Barr walked into the office.

"Thank you for that." he said. "I heard you on the 'phone. That was a brilliant answer. I knew I could trust you to take charge."

"Sit down." I said as I pulled up another office chair by my desk. What's happened?"

He began to sob uncontrollably. I had never experienced a grown man in a position of responsibility lose his cool composure in such a way. He held on to me and wept on my shoulder. Through his tears he spoke disjointedly.

"He's gone, you know . . . . Darren . . . . the accident . . . his motorbike . . . he didn't stand a chance . . . . he's gone . . . it's all over . . . . everything's over . . . . Darren, . . . my marriage . . . . I'm glad I've got you . . . . I lean on you . . . . I can talk to you . . . ."

He looked up at me. He was a broken man. I didn't know what to say. I couldn't comfort him. I was shocked by the news of Darren's sudden death. I wanted to now how it had happened and where but didn't like to ask for details. He had been my 'boyfriend' for a short time. That was how I had got to know the De-Barrs.

The telephone rang again. I answered it. It was the same reporter wanting news of the accident. I didn't answer. I put down the 'phone and went to the cupboard. This was a crisis. Nigel would have made a cup of tea. Mr. De-Barr needed something stronger and I knew where the whisky was kept. I poured him a glass and he downed it in one breath then handed me the glass for a refill. I poured another but refused to give him a third.

"What would I do without you?" he said. "You look after me. You know I'm very fond of you Laura don't you. Ever since that day when Darren brought you back to the house and you told me your sad life story, I've wanted to look after you but here you are looking after me. My marriage is over and now I've lost my youngest son. *You* won't let me down will you?"

I thought of my plans to leave and set up a business of my own but this was not the time to tell him. I telephoned Nigel and explained all that had happened.

"Please Nigel, can you come round to the office with the car and give Mr. De-Barr a lift home? He's not in a fit state to drive. I'm coming home too. I need you. There's nothing we can do here. Please Love. I'll see you soon."

Late than evening I sat at home with Nigel and told him all that happened. We had more details of the accident. It was on the local television news. A van had skidded and ran into Darren's bike. There were witnesses. It wasn't his fault. It was all over so quickly. He didn't suffer for long. I talked to Nigel about my plans to leave the job and set up on my own.

"I can't leave him now. He says he needs me."

"You've got your own life to lead. You must make your own decision."

"But he's been so good to me, to both of us. He's trained me and taught me so much about mortgages and finance. He's paid to send me on courses. I can't let him down."

"You're not letting him down. You've worked for him for over six years now. Yeah! He's been good to you but just think, you've been good to him. You've kept the business going when he was on holiday or away or down the pub. All those Saturday mornings when you went in to clean and sort the post. You've been very good."

"I don't know what to do."

"You'd already made up your mind to leave. Just because Darren's died you don't have to change your life. Go on, be brave! Hand in your notice. He's loaded anyway. He doesn't need the money . . . and we do. It's only fair."

Put like that it seemed to make sense.

Over the next few days I took advice myself on starting a business. I spoke to others who had made the same decision. It was exciting and encouraging. I knew that I could do it. All the work that I had done for the De-Barrs. Instead of putting more money into their pockets I could help us. We did need the money. Here was I offering mortgage advice to others and then going home to our rented accommodation.

The following Monday morning I asked Mr. De-Barr if I could have a word with him in his office. He invited me in and I sat down, took a deep breath and said,

"Mr. De-Barr, you have been very good to me over the years and I really appreciate it but I have made a decision. I wish to hand in my notice."

There was a stunned silence for a moment then he began to laugh.

"Oh, yes! Very funny! Well no, it's not funny. Where do you think you could get another job like this?"

"I'm going to start my own business."

"Doing what? Selling flowers? Oh yeah! You could be a lady in a flower shop just like Eliza Doolittle." he laughed again.

"No. I'm going to start a finance company. That's what you have taught me. That's what I know. I've thought about it for ages. Nigel and I have talked about it. I've made up my mind Mr. De-Barr. I'm sorry if I am letting you down. I really . . ."

"Letting me down?" he interrupted angrily. "I've done a lot for you Madam and this is how you repay me, and just when I need you most."

"You don't need me here in the office. When I go you won't need to replace me so you'll save money. It could help the company."

"But I need you. I need someone to talk to."

"I hope we shall still be friends. We can still talk."

"I need you." His voice began to crack. I wasn't sure whether he was angry or upset. "I need you. I have lost everything. Everything! My marriage is over, my son has gone, my business is failing. If you go I shall have nothing else left to live for."

"But you still have your family."

"I have neglected my family in order to build up the business. Now I have neither."

"The business will pick up. This is just a temporary blip."

"My dear girl, this is not a 'temporary blip' as you say. My life is ruined. If you go too, . . . I have no reason to live."

"I've made up my mind Mr. De-Barr. I wish to hand in my notice. Here is my letter of resignation." He put his hands up to his face and hung his head, so I placed the letter deliberately on his desk. "Thank you for all your help and support Mr. De-Barr. I think it best if I leave immediately. I will clear my desk and go now. Good bye."

He didn't reply.

CHAPTER 29

He was found the next morning. He had taken a massive overdose of his medication. I had underestimated his threats. I had no idea he really meant it. People say these things but they never mean it, not really. I was devastated and definitely in no mood to start a new company. I had lost all enthusiasm for the project. I tried to talk to Nigel and explain how I felt but he didn't understand.

"I thought you were all keen on this business thing. It would have meant more money for us, for you and me. You've handed in your notice. You can't go back on that. Besides . . . I've had an idea too."

"And what's your idea?" I wasn't really listening to him.

"I'm going to get a new job too!"

I sat up suddenly. "A new job? Where?"

"I've handed in my notice too and I'm going to be a bus driver. I saw a notice on the back of a bus and it said,

'YOU COULD BE DRIVING THIS BUS.'

So I went along to the depot and they want to see me on Monday morning. I handed in my notice straight away. That's it! I've left that old place and I'm going to be a bus-driver."

"But you haven't got the job yet! You shouldn't have handed in your notice."

"Why not? You did! Anyway, I shall get the job of

driving a bus. It's no different from driving a car, just a bit bigger that's all."

"Of course it's different. You're crazy! You have to know all the routes and the timetables and collect the fares and give change and look after the passengers and . . . . oh,—all sorts of stuff."

"Yeah! Well . . . . O.K. . . . but they want to see me Monday morning. That's good isn't it? I'll be great at driving buses just you see."

Monday morning came and Nigel found it was not quite as simple as he had expected. He had to fill in lots of forms and he wasn't very good at that. I usually helped him with paper work. He had an interview and then an examination on basic mathematics and map reading and understanding timetables. It took all day and he didn't even get to drive a bus. He was fed up when he got home. A few days later there came a letter saying his application had been unsuccessful.

So now we were both out of work. The only solution was for me to go back to the idea of starting my own business. One morning I met a colleague from De-Barr's company. She and I went for a coffee in town. By the end of our conversation we were partners, setting up a financial advisory company. Having a partner was just the inspiration I needed. We worked together well. We had different strengths. She was a few years older than me. Her experience coupled with my youth and enthusiasm we made a good team. I had some money left to me following the death of my father that I ploughed straight into the new venture. There was so much to plan. Pat and I met every day that week and talked and planned and laughed and cried together. She had worked in finance even longer than I had. With Mr. De-Barr's suicide, the company was closing down. We could take over their clients. It sounded mercenary but this was business. At the end of a week we bought a bottle of champagne and toasted the launch of

'HARVEY AND GILBERT CO. LTD.—FINANCIAL ADVISORS.'

The names 'Harvey and Gilbert' were not our names at all. We just thought they sounded honest, reliable and very English; good names for financial advisors.

One evening I was sitting at home relaxing with Nigel and chatting to him about our plans when he suddenly interrupted me. He shouted:

"Pat this, and Pat that! All I hear about is Pat, Pat, Pat! I'm fed up with it. You see more of her than you do of me. Can't you talk about something else for a change."

"I'm sorry Love! I don't mean to go on about it. I'm just very excited about it. Until you get another job we need to get our business up and running. We need to start making some money."

"And that's another thing! You've used all that money that was left to us. It's all gone . . . just because *Pat* says."

I tried to remain calm. "It was my money. It was left to *me* by my family to spend as I wanted. It was mine."

"I thought it was *ours*. We are married you know."

"Then you must get out there and start supporting us. *You* be the bread-winner!"

We were having our first real row. I tried to appease the situation by changing the subject.

"Nigel," I said in my quiet, mysterious voice. "Nigel, have you noticed anything?"

153

"I've noticed we're having a row."

"No, have you noticed anything about me?"

"Like what?"

"Have you noticed anything different about me?"

"I've noticed you've become a stroppy old thing, if that's what you mean."

"No really, Love, something very important and different"

He stopped and looked at me carefully. He eyed me up and down.

"You've had your hair done?" he asked questioningly.

"No I haven't. It's more important than that."

"Oh I wish you wouldn't ask me silly things like this. You know I never notice things. You'll have to tell me."

"Well, ... I haven't had a fit for eight weeks!"

"Really? That's amazing! Well actually I had noticed, I just didn't like to say anything in case it made you think about fits and then you'd have one."

"Oh yes?" I joked. "You're trying to tell me that you **had** noticed. I'm not sure that I believe you." I laughed and he laughed with me. "What with all the stress we've been under recently. It's the longest I've ever been without a seizure."

"Must be wedded bliss!" he laughed.

And the row was forgotten . . . . for a while at least.

CHAPTER 30

Sometimes, when a dream comes true it turns out to be a nightmare. Marriage to Nigel had been my dream from that first crazy day when I watched him from my bedroom window; the silly school days when I sat in class signing my name with his on my school books; the evenings when I would relax on the bed in my room thinking of him and then that first scrappy note posted through the letter box when he thought my name was Lolly-Pop! It all seems so long ago and I find it hard to remember my childhood. Were there any happy times?

Nigel and I were very different. I had grown up. I was strong, ambitious and determined. I had a dream. He just lived in a dream world.

I would have liked to have children but it didn't happen. I knew I could conceive easily, it had happened before when it wasn't planned so I told him it must be his fault. I told Mary that he was 'firing blanks'. The marriage lasted five years.

*   *   *

Now I am married to Stuart. We've been together eight years. We 'flew away' to a secret rendez-vous in the Grand Canyon. It was wonderfully romantic. I didn't even invite the family. Mary and Len are not my family. I don't have any real family. I always longed for REAL family. My mother has been gone so long I sometimes find it hard to remember what she was like. Memories come and go in short flashes like scenes in a film. No-one came to our wedding. Not even Andrew. It was just Stuart and me. I wore a white dress trimmed with pink and lilac lace. I carried a huge bouquet of white roses and the sun shone warm on our union. Stuart is so good to me. He has taken me to places I had only dreamed about. I have experienced a whole new way of life.

I still hear news of Nigel. He's married with four children. Stuart and I will have children too. One day. It **will** happen. I'm sure it will. They will be my family. I would love a baby girl and name her after my mother. Katy is married with three children. David is married with two little girls. Andrew is married with a baby son. We have all grown apart and I rarely see them. Stuart is my family now and when we have children I will concentrate on them. I shall dedicate my life to them. I will make sure they have a happy childhood. I never knew that joy.

The finance business did well for a short while. Well enough for me to be able to get onto the property ladder. Pat and I got on when things were going well but there's a credit crunch, a serious recession so our business folded. We got out at the right time. I have a job in an office near to our house. It's easier that way. I don't have epileptic fits any more but I don't have very good health either. I try to stay healthy so that I will conceive and have my longed for family. I eat salads and fruit. I've lost a lot of weight. People say I look pale and tired. I work hard.

* * *

CHAPTER 31

As I sit at the computer writing these last pages my hand goes to my rounding belly and I fondly caress the longed-for baby within. She is my daughter. She makes me smile. At last I shall experience the mother/daughter relationship once more. I shall know how my mother felt about me. Our family line will continue. My future is secure. Already she is mine. Her name is Rosie-Louise. I have found my angel.

*   *   *

If this were fiction, it would have a nice, neat ending, but life is not like that. My pregnancy lasted three months. The doctor said there was no real reason for a miscarriage and if I stay healthy I could conceive again.

Mary once said to me,

"If your life story was written down in a book no-one would believe it."

But this is not fiction.

CODA

That was all so long ago. So long ago. My life has moved on.

Jack is my beautiful, blue-eyed son. He is two years old. I watch him now giggling and splashing in the puddles with his wellington boots. Jack and me. Just the two of us. I never knew I could love so much.

Is this how my mother felt about me?

Lightning Source UK Ltd.
Milton Keynes UK
UKOW03f2357030414

229396UK00001B/9/P

9 781491 898734